SHAME THE DEVIL

BOOKS BY PHILIP APPLEMAN

FICTION

Shame the Devil
In the Twelfth Year of the War

•

POETRY

Open Doorways
Summer Love and Surf
Kites on a Windy Day

•

NONFICTION

The Silent Explosion

•

EDITED WORKS

Darwin
An Essay on the Principle of Population
The Origin of Species
1859: Entering an Age of Crisis (coeditor)

SHAME THE DEVIL

a novel by
Philip Appleman

A Herbert Michelman Book
Crown Publishers, Inc.
New York

Library of Congress Cataloging in Publication Data
Appleman, Philip, 1926–
Shame the devil
"A Herbert Michelman book."
I. Title.
PS3551.P6S5   1981   813'.54   80-22966
ISBN: 0-517-542862

Design: Deborah B. Kerner

10 9 8 7 6 5 4 3 2 1
First edition

FOR MARGIE

... when I try to imagine a faultless love
Or the life to come, what I hear is the murmur
Of underground streams, what I see is a limestone landscape.
—W. H. AUDEN

From Odin's name came the name Audun.
—THE YNGLINGA SAGA

Tell truth, and shame the devil.
—HOTSPUR

SHAME THE DEVIL

ONE

SHIFTY as a shortstop, the Stingray swung in for gas at the outskirts of town. Somewhere behind were the relentless agents, somewhere ahead all that fool's gold and the nagging mysteries of J. Randolph Wong. Uncle Julian could take sports cars or leave them (over the hill, he was over the hill), but Frank was hooked on that rumble and rhythm, and never got tired behind the wheel. So they had done it all—the Garden State, the Keystone State, the Buckeye State, the Hoosier State—all in one sitting, rest stops excluded, the bulky Julian wedged in the death seat, talking nonstop, while Frank eased up and down on the accelerator, watching his chances, hitting the brake for pushy semi's, veering and weaving: eight hundred miles of hustle.

"Pagans, Frank, the Vikings were pagans till the twelfth century, think of it, and by then the long ships had raided every coastal town and monastery worth trashing, in France, Germany, Britain. Imagine the loot—golden chalices, silver bowls, jeweled medallions, ancient coins. Heathen hordes from the North, leaving their runic graffiti scrawled across marble temples like public toilets, as far south as Greece, Byzantium."

"Twenty hours flat," Frank announced. "Could have made it in sixteen if it hadn't been for the traffic jams."

On the Jaguar ahead of them a Dayglo bumper sticker gleamed crimson.

WHEN GUNS ARE OUTLAWED
ONLY OUTLAWS WILL HAVE GUNS

Frank sniffed; the gas fumes cheered him. He wrinkled his nose, savoring that perfume: high-octane premium, and the fragrance of new tires, and the musky leather of bucket seats.

It was a short line, only four cars ahead of them, and soon the Stingray slid up to the pump. Frank switched off the engine and eased out, stretching his arms and legs voluptuously, like a relief pitcher. Grit settled out of the sky and crusted the silver car. While a kid in blue jeans filled the tank, Frank flicked soot off the Simoniz.

Inside the station Julian was pumping the candy machine for Hershey bars. He ate a big meal four or five times a day and snacked heavily in between, especially when he was working, writing, his restless brain clamoring for calories. "Spoilers of Lindisfarne," he called, lumbering back to the car, "plunderers of London and Hamburg, Paris and Seville. And after all that, the best museums have only scrounged up a few kilos of Viking coins, some of their arm rings, brooches, cups, jeweled bucklers—tokens, mere tokens. Where's all the rest of it?"

Frank patted the hot hood absently. He was missing Nancy already, more than he'd ever expected to.

Munching almonds, Julian's voice was rich with chocolate and passion. "Charles the Bald, ransomed with seven hundred pounds of gold, forty thousand pounds of silver. All those centuries of piracy, pillage, slave-running, the world's greatest international blackmailers, they must have ripped off a mountain of gold, and it's all out here somewhere, shiploads of it."

Frank snorted. "In these cornfields?" A storm of old newspapers blew past. Flapping his arms like a clown, he freed himself from a comic section. Somewhere back there on the glutted interstate, the agents were gaining on them. He imagined them in black sedans, lean and slit-eyed under their snap-brim Dick Tracy hats. He got back in the driver's seat as Julian squeezed his girth into the other side.

"But their gold isn't the point." Julian was licking chocolate off his fingers, sly as a cat. "No, the big questions are still out there, too, all the old imponderables. How do the great gods vanish? Freyr the Sun, Odin the Sky-father, Freya, Thor, the Valkyries. What cavern holds the fettered Loki now?"

Frank snaked the car back into traffic. "I still say it's bananas, this whole trip. Norse gods? Gold? Now? A thousand years afterwards? In Indiana?" But Frank knew it was useless to protest. Julian had picked up the Viking bug, an incurable malady.

Besides, Julian made a practice of ignoring anything he didn't want to hear, and lately that included most of what Frank had to say. "Where is Valhalla now? Where are the roots of Yggdrasil, the sacred ash that binds the universe? In our dreams, yes, in our old tales, in the urges and terrors of our sleeping minds, of course. But it's not enough, Frank. There's more than that out here somewhere, and somehow Wong has got his lucky, greedy hands on all of it." Julian burped, staccato: a sign of deep frustration.

"Wong, schmong, I've been hearing that for eight hundred miles. This is the wildest goose chase yet."

If their whole aggressive operation slid into bankruptcy, it would be that furtive Hoosier's fault: J. Randolph Wong. Was it his real name, an inscrutable midwestern Oriental? Or just a clumsy alias? Why did he keep switching his return address, post office boxes in three different towns? Wong had more straight dope on the Vikings than anyone Julian had ever come across, and the trail of his runic parchments led, deviously, to Ash Garden, Indiana.

They passed a Lions Club welcome sign.

ASH GARDEN
TOWN WITH A PAST, CITY OF THE FUTURE

Frank played the Stingray past a double row of ancient ash trees that no doubt gave the town its name, past the yellow blinkers of auto salesrooms and used-car lots, past the stone gates of a public park, where bulldozers were uprooting trees, past the concrete banks of a river, foamy as beer, past a coal-burning power plant, its smokestacks pumping a brown odor into the thickening sky, past dozens of billboards.

PROTECT OUR ENVIRONMENT
DON'T LITTER

BE SURE, BE SECURE
FATHER MAGNUS FOR SHERIFF

PLAY IT SAFE
RE-ELECT SHERIFF OLAF

Colossal faces of the two candidates glared down at the creeping traffic.

". . . so Leif the Lucky sailed westward from Helluland, finding vines and grapes, skies blue as sapphires, streams rushing pure to the sea, and then westward again to Labrador, to Newfoundland. And then?" Julian paused with one hand raised like an orator. "We need Wong, my boy, as much as he needs us. We can't leave everything hanging in midair." Julian's mellow voice was suddenly strained; he was hunching forward in his seat, wistfully watching the McDonalds and Arbys and Dairy Queens slide by.

"Why not?" Frank began to look for a motel. *Why not, why not?* Julian had gone off on tangents before, plenty of them, but Frank had never seen him this compulsive. Still, after four years of partnership, he knew there was a lot more to his erratic uncle than the two hundred and ninety pounds that met the eye.

Broncos and Colts, Torinos and Mavericks, Pintos and Mustangs were jockeying for advantage on the bumpy street. A couple of teenagers in an old green Barracuda pulled alongside and stayed there, revving furiously, challenging the Stingray. Frank grinned at the kids indulgently, seeing himself a few years back, barreling down the Old Post Road, on the berm at the right or in an occasional gap across the double yellow line, facing the oncoming lanes with lights and blinkers on, the miracle of an open stretch, a thousand yards of vacuum, blood pounding in the temples, dodging back at the last possible moment to the indignant braking shriek of middle-aged vans and station wagons.

His toes acted on their own, pressing the insole. The silver hood edged up, one yard from the bumper ahead of him. He felt the surging power under his shoe: four hundred sixty foot-pounds of torque, five hundred fifty horsepower, a hundred forty miles an hour in seventeen seconds flat, the seven-litre L-88 brutal and potent, pulsing now in feral anticipation. Frank suddenly realized that he had a throbbing erection. He caught a glimpse of Nancy's long dark hair. Embarrassed, he eased up on his accelerator foot. Too old for that kid stuff. Twenty-four. God.

Forget it.

The teenagers gave him the finger and squeezed through traffic, looking for a live one, their battered fenders daring other fenders and winning. The Barracuda slithered farther and farther ahead, finally out of sight.

Frank relaxed. The erection was gone.

The billboards became more frequent.

ASHLAND COUNTY FAIR
OLD-TIME FUN FOR EVERYONE

The pavement was a maze of shredded truck tires, dead mufflers, and tail pipes. Traffic was slowing down, most drivers dutifully leaning on their horns. Shotguns and rifles glinted in rear-window gun racks. Eighteen-wheelers threw their weight around, hogging the passing lane. On the berm a police car flashed by, axles pounding like pistons, the siren driving needles in Frank's head. He thought of the snap-brimmed agents somewhere behind them, and felt his hands go slippery on the wheel. Why hadn't they moved in? "No case," Julian always said. "They haven't got a case, not the F.B.I. As far as they're concerned, you can commit the same offense in all fifty states separately, just not in any two simultaneously. That's federalism."

"Yes, but haven't we done it in two states simultaneously?" Frank suddenly put it aloud to Julian, who fielded the question on the first bounce.

"You mean because of Wong? I avoided any entangling alliances with him while we were still in New York. Now that we're across the Hoosier state line, I'll put him under contract fast enough. If we find him."

There was the federal law against using the mails to defraud, of course. But defrauding whom, Julian always asked, a question to which there seemed to be no statutory answer. Apparently it was not even a misdemeanor to write a doctoral dissertation for someone else.

And that was their vocation, Julian's and Frank's: Confidential Services, Inc., Ed.D. dissertations for all comers, on ten days' notice.

Four years, now, of dissertations: drab work, but profitable. "Education is richly rewarding," Frank would call out to Nancy, on his way to the bank. Julian could dictate the rough draft of an Ed.D. dissertation in two or three days, concocting the stuff entirely out of his head. And because he produced a fabricated New England study for the doctoral candidate from Buffalo ("The Film Loop as Homiletic Device in Rhode Island Vocational Schools") or a fictitious Iowa investigation for the candidate from Albany ("Comparative Analyses of the Peer-Group Attitudes of Random Des Moines Overachievers"), it was a simple feat to create plausible statistics that would never be checked.

The trouble was that Uncle Julian, for all his brilliance of invention, was not a steady man. Pushing fifty-five but showing no signs of slowing down, he still got carried away—by girls a third his age, by older women, by pretty boys. But worse than that, far worse, was his inability to control himself in the presence of an idea. Ideas seduced him easily and often, and once taken in, Julian was lost to common sense, driven by some freakish convolution in the frontal lobes. The dissertation business at such times was always abandoned, a casualty of his infatuation.

And therefore J. Randolph Wong and the Vikings. And therefore this insane excursion to the boondocks of Indiana. Frank felt a sneaky twinge of fear. There was something unnerving about this whole crazy project. He couldn't shake off the feeling that if they ever did find Wong, it would be the most unlucky discovery of their lives.

The motel sign caught Frank's eye, almost too late to make the turn. The Stingray plunged over the low curb and into the last free parking slot. Frank patted the wheel, switched off the motor, and glanced at the blinking neon.

The crudely outlined animals flashed on and off, on and off, deep red in the late afternoon murk. A fire truck screamed by, cars squeezing lanes to make room. Frank shouted, "This look OK?"

The leonine head nodded absently. They got out, locked up, and crossed the hot blacktop to the motel office.

What are we doing here? Frank's good sense came at him with a whip. Just what the hell are we doing out here in the sticks?

Truth, Julian would say. The truth, wholeness.

The office door shut itself to the deprecating tinkle of a little brass bell. There was no one around. Julian called out, "Anybody home?"

"Hold your goddam water, I'm coming."

And soon they entered from a back room: a middle-aged woman, once clearly a beauty but now weighing in at about two hundred, and a slight blond girl wearing jeans and a red plaid shirt. The girl seemed angry at something, glancing at Frank and Julian as if they were a public nuisance. She wasn't especially pretty, but when she glared at Frank, his belly muscles did quick, involuntary calisthenics.

"Have a good time at the fair, Moonchild. Enjoy your companions, be sincere. But keep your feelings to yourself. And don't trust any shitty Pisces, you hear?"

"OK, Mama, OK." She moved slowly toward the door, head down as if in a sulk, her walk slightly off balance, almost awkward. She carried her arms away from her sides, palms out, her fingers caressing things as she passed—the desk top, a chair, the television—little gestures of innocence, of endless experience. Frank wrenched himself from paralysis and spoke.

"Is it far from here, the fair?"

"Walking distance," the big woman boomed. "Everybody's welcome."

This time the girl looked at him with a sideways glance—shy, or cunning—and the pink mouth made words: "Come. Yes, come." Was it an invitation? A challenge? Her goodbye was another frown, but when her blue eyes met Frank's, his insides turned marshmallow. He disgusted himself.

He thought of Nancy's dark eyes, her brown hair rippling on saffron sheets.

Julian ordered adjoining rooms and got the last pair in the house. While he wrote in the register, their genial hostess made conversation.

". . . name's Sybil," she was saying, "but just call me Fat Mama, everybody does. Here for the fair, are you?" She winked a lot when she talked, as if every word were a confidence.

"Why, yes. My nephew and I are on vacation. Thought we'd just stop by for it."

"Well, it beats hell out of all the others around here. The election parade's always a gasser, it's on tonight, you ought to go, what're your birthdays?"

"I beg your pardon?"

"Your birthdays." She peered at Julian. "You're a Taurus, aren't you?"

Julian was getting that odd, squinty look, his intrigued look. Frank tensed. They had enough trouble already, what with Wong and the agents and the Vikings. Nip it in the bud, stop the nonsense. "That's right," he blurted. "He's a Taurus."

Julian glanced at Frank, annoyed, and Frank grinned back at him as if he'd just stolen second.

"I knew it. Mars in the seventh house, Pluto trine the ascendant. I'm never wrong, it's a gift." Her husky voice went lower, conspiratorial. "Listen, don't be afraid to confide in strangers this week." She winked at Julian. He still had that odd look, his eyes glazing.

Frank was alarmed. There was something puzzling behind her playful wink and the astrological prattle. He tried to divert her from Julian. "And me?"

Her head came around smoothly, as if on ball bearings. "Gemini," she said firmly. He nodded. Why not? "Venus transiting Aries, I can always tell." She winked.

Frank felt foolish, weary. Twenty hours of driving. He stared at his shoes.

"Look for opportunities today, Gemini. Be ready to grab the bull by the horns, take chances, proceed with caution, take nothing for granted."

The tone wasn't right, the inflections off. She wasn't listening to her own voice. Frank glanced up.

She was holding Julian's hand, her free fingers tracing lines across his palm. "Do you believe in soul mates? In fate? In love at first sight?" she murmured. "Give romance a chance today. Put those little scruples aside. This is a time of surprises, adventure, good fortune."

Julian burped softly.

Waves of road-weariness swept over Frank in the glaze of Julian's eyes. He knew all the next moves; he couldn't stop it now.

"I'll be in my room." Grabbing his key, he stumbled out the tinkling door and across the steamy blacktop, and somewhere fell on a bed, asleep before the chenille had pressed parallel creases across his face.

TWO

THE THUNDER in Frank's dream was Julian, dropping an armful of books on the floor of the adjoining room. The connecting door was open.

"On your feet, boy, we're going to the fair. Old-time fun for everyone."

Frank couldn't believe it. He rolled over, face to the wall.

"Come on, help me get the car unloaded. We're going out on the town. On the double."

Frank was almost asleep again, but heard and resisted. "What time is it, for God's sake?"

"Never mind what time it is, you've had your little nap, now hustle before we miss the fair entirely. You lose your taste for cotton candy?"

Frank groaned and with a massive effort opened his eyes. His watch fuzzed into focus. Eight o'clock. He'd only been asleep three hours. Julian was bustling around. Frank recognized his familiar postcoital elation: Julian had laid the fat woman.

A second stack of books hit the floor. Julian's hobby was speed-reading scholarly tomes, monographs in three languages, the more arcane the better. He had read hundreds of them in the four years they had worked together. He even remembered what was in them, and consequently gave the irritating impression of knowing everything.

Still in a daze, Frank watched him go out again and waddle back in with their two small suitcases. "Listen, Julian, I'm shot. If you want to go to that fair, go ahead, but I'm staying right here in this room, and in this bed. Close the door, will you?"

Julian paused in his work, solemn. "My boy, I promised your father I would do everything in my power to promote your best interests— *don't mouth those words with me, son, this is serious*—and that is what I have always done and will continue to do. At the moment, your best interest is at the fair. It's a golden opportunity to do some snooping after J. Randolph Wong."

"Can't you forget him for a few hours and let me get some sleep? Close the door, damn it!"

He got up and closed it himself.

"As long as you're up, give me a hand here." Julian was arranging the books alphabetically by author: compulsively neat, as might be expected of a man who had ghostwritten two hundred dissertations in four years.

The projects came to them in every state of promise and disarray, some half-finished, victims of mysterious writers' blocks or of inhuman teaching loads at shabby schools, others hardly more than the original twinkle in the candidate's eye, prospectuses and noble hopes. But then Julian would improvise his plausible statistics, and Frank would transform them into the patois of Educationese, and Nancy, the resident financial wizard, would neatly launder the income, and lo, another five thou was on its way to the bank.

Oh lovely Nancy with all the virtues. And a very large and very hostile husband.

"Here it is." Julian was holding the provocative, unfinished dissertation of J. Randolph Wong, allegedly a doctoral candidate at Southern Indiana University, and a challenge to Julian, a challenge so compelling that the smooth cursive of their lives had been hopelessly smudged. He fondled the slender manuscript, his own translation from the Viking parchments that Wong had sent him, and an original contribution to knowledge, Julian always said, if there ever was one.

He began reading. " 'The breeze was fair and easterly, and at long last we sighted the nameless coast . . .' "

Frank felt the tug of Wong's mystery, but he resented its breaking into their busy, prosperous lives. He scuttled off to the bathroom and locked the door, but still he could hear Julian's sonorous voice.

" 'Of the twenty ships at sailing, only seventeen had survived the cruel voyage, but we were still a mighty force, and feared nothing but failure in our quest for the central cave. We sighted first the reefs, then, by dead reckoning south, the great river itself, bearing the brown gift of freshness to the spiteful sea. We were half a day's journey upriver before the darkness forced us to ship oars and cast anchor. There in the twilight, I myself in solemn celebration sacrificed one of the seven bound bulls brought from the homeland. Seizing the beast by the nostrils, in the manner of our mysteries, my right hand plunged the sacred knife into the black bull's heart.' "

Sacred knives. Black bulls. Seeing his face in the bathroom mirror, Frank realized, with a thrill of self-loathing, that he was hanging on every word, fascinated.

" 'The chiefs, assembled in my long ship, gathered round in the flickering light of our ritual torches, and passed the hollow skull of steaming blood. Arrayed in our seven holy orders, we drank to the defeat of the spirit of darkness, to the mystery of ever-renewing life, to our hunt for the central cave, somewhere in the woods, the sacred ash trees of the West.

" 'That night the holy slaughter renewed our strength. The air was fresh off the virgin land, the river ran sweet past our tight hulls. The stars in their alien heavens, the clean wind in the primal forest gathered round us in praise, the veiled forces of creation guiding us to our promised haven, deep in the bosom of our mother.' "

Frank found himself listening breathlessly, ear to the bathroom door. Embarrassing. The door banged open as his indignation poured through the adjoining rooms. "Bosom of our mother! Who needs it, Julian? Weren't we doing all right in New York? Four dissertations, twenty G's a month? My father always said, when you're making it, don't ask questions. And here we are out in some weird little cow town . . ."

"Not only a compelling document in itself," Julian was musing, "but breathtaking in its suggestions. How in the world did Wong come across all this Viking parchment? What is the central cave? Why won't he tell us? Why doesn't he answer my queries?"

"My father knew the value of a dollar. He knew the value of a hundred thousand a year after taxes. He knew about depletion allowances, long-term capital gains, accelerated depreciation. He never in his life asked about my 'best interests,' because he knew where my best interests were, in high yields, that's where, in . . ."

"Why won't Wong give me his home address? Why do we have to track him down by triangulating from his various post office boxes? And what's all that Mickey Mouse—'mysteries'? 'Mother'? What kind of talk is that for Vikings?"

"Nose to the grindstone, that's my best interest. Lettuce, bread, the long green. My father knew that."

"What's Wong keeping from us? What's the truth of the matter? Frank, my boy, this may be the one we've waited for all these years, the real contribution, the one that will heal us, make us whole again."

"I'm whole, I'm whole, I'm a free agent, I've still got a healthy respect for the buck. You're the one who's coming unglued, translating runes, for God's sake!" Frank was already tired of his own indignation, ashamed of his shouting. He was also just plain tired. Weary. Profit and loss. "Anyway, I'm not going to any grungy county fair."

But as usual he gave in, and soon Julian was elbowing through the crowds with Frank trudging in his wake. At every corner bonfires were blazing, sending showers of sparks down the darkening streets. Young women, garlanded in red plastic flowers, danced around the bonfires. Small boys dared each other and leaped over the tall flames, shrieking.

"Midsummer Eve." Julian was getting excited. "The heavenly sun retreats to his cold death again, the yearly cycle turns, festivals of fire tend the dying flame of heaven. Goes back a long time—beyond memory, beyond history. 'Balder's Fires' they call them in Sweden.

Scare the trolls away. The Vikings may have kindled them in the New World. We're on the right track here."

The homely scene menaced Frank. Omens slithered out of the smoke, tickling the back of his neck. They passed the public park again, where dozens of people had chained themselves to tree trunks, chanting "Save the trees! Save our park! Save the trees!" A construction billboard announced: SUNRISE PARK: FUTURE HOME OF THE SUNRISE PARKING LOT.

At the seventh eye-watering bonfire, he was ready to give it up. "Walking distance means three blocks, maximum, everybody knows that. Why didn't we drive?" Deprived of the Stingray, he felt vulnerable.

"We're in the provinces. Folks still do a little hiking out here."

FEEL SECURE
RE-ELECT SHERIFF BIG OLAF

the huge billboards repeated. And

SAFETY   SANCTITY   SCORPIO
FATHER MAGNUS FOR SHERIFF

The faces of the two candidates glowered down at them, repetitious as Xerox between the constant admonitions:

KEEP ASH GARDEN BEAUTIFUL
DON'T LITTER

And spray-painted on the sides of buildings:

SAVE SUNRISE PARK

Finally the sound of calliopes greeted them faintly, then the chain-saw whine of the drag track. At the fairground gates Frank caught his breath. Overhead a custom Panther V-12 sedan was rotating majestically, enshrined on a tall turntable, its golden finish glistening in the slowly changing hues of powerful spotlights. The crowd gazed at it silently, adoring young faces in the reflected light turning slowly red then yellow then green.

"Seven hundred b.h.p., archetypal," Julian said drily. "Deep in the American soul is the totem of the thousand-horsepower car, the goal and image of all our earnest striving. Gas shortages can't dim that vision, subcompacts can't kill it, no, the dream lives on like the midsummer fires, like Yggdrasil itself, it lives, survives."

Frank knew Julian was sneering, but he felt tears in his eyes. Slowly they passed through the glittering gates. Looking back, he caught a last hungry glimpse of the Panther; lust gathered in his throat.

Bonfires were everywhere in the fairgrounds, kids leaping over them with eager shouts. As Frank and Julian plodded the midway, bright banners fluttered around them, and the fortissimo roar of the rides and games was a nostalgic touch of Manhattan. Frank's persistent tenseness irritated him. He took a deep breath and smiled at a pretty girl, but she didn't smile back. Something in her manner flashed him a subliminal glimpse of the aggressive Jessie Bell, freshman amazon, who once upon a time had done him wrong. He looked away, feeling vaguely guilty, and they walked on.

Midway crowds bumped sociably at their hips and shoulders as they passed from booth to booth, finally stopping at the cockfighting tent. There were no signs to identify the candy-striped pavilion, but Julian knew what was going on.

"There's one at every fair, Frank. Playboys and proles, bankers and debutantes, they all love it. Strictly illegal, of course. Look over there."

Frank hadn't noticed: behind the ticket taker, unobtrusive, a sheriff's deputy was tallying the receipts. Julian grinned. "Law and order in Ashland County. Old-time fun for everyone. Including J. Randolph Wong, maybe? Let's just see if we spot any exotic eyelids in there, or skin the color of oolong."

They paid and squeezed their way inside. The birds were fighting with a combination of gaffs on one spur and slashers on the other, wicked-looking, razor-sharp blades, like little sabers. They circled each other, leaping and fanning in midair. Young people around the pit were screaming for the red bird, older ones for the blue. There was a flurry in the pit, and the blue cock pecked savagely at the red one's head, plucking out an eye. The older people cheered, but their joy was brief. The red cock leaped straight into the air, fanned furiously, and came down with his needle-pointed spur thrust deep into the blue bird's thigh. Frank winced and shut his eyes, a sympathetic stabbing in his leg.

The young fans were cheering, but the fight wasn't over; the blue cock wrenched free and sent a flurry of fierce thumping kicks at the red, and the slasher struck, cutting steel across the craw, leaving the red head dangling, the unlucky bird scuttling zigzag in a spraying of blood. Amid victory yelps and muttered curses, money changed hands around the ring.

Frank had had enough. He led Julian away, out of the tent, into the stream of cheery faces. At the next booth, Julian paused in his quest for Oriental complexions long enough to throw a few bowie knives, aiming for a man who poked his head through a hole in the back wall of the booth. The man kept ducking smartly, his cap a thick wooden bull's-eye that absorbed the wicked points. Three hits in the cap won a pearl-handled switchblade. This particular target was an old-timer, a couple of thick scars on his cheeks but casually skillful, taunting the players, grinning and bobbing and ducking in his tight circumference, always getting his head down in time. Challenged, Frank picked up a knife.

Close to his ear, the stranger's voice was insinuating. "A little competition? To make it interesting? Say, ten bucks a toss?"

Frank went rigid, staring at the snap-brim hat and the sinister half-smile. A fifteen-inch blade slapped flat and easy against a palm.

"Just a little competition? Friendly, of course."

A dozen teenagers swept between them and the stranger, transistors blaring. Panicky, Frank pulled Julian into the ripple and flow of the crowd.

"Some other time, then." The genial voice hung in the air like smoke. Frank looked back. He was still standing there in his neat necktie and his Dick Tracy hat, slapping the bowie knife in his palm. Suddenly he whirled and threw at the grinning target: strike. Frank tugged Julian into a fast walk. "Let's get the hell away from here!"

But Julian, compulsive sleuth, wasn't ready to give up his search for Wong. He dragged to a halt and pointed. "Look." On a nearby hill were two floodlighted steeples, the twin white fingers of an imposing church, pointing to zenith.

"Stone-age country. A high place. A mere two hundred years ago this land was Neolithic. Ten thousand years in a glance, think of it. Whatever Wong has to say, whatever he has to hide . . ."

Frank tried to keep calm. He didn't want to get tangled again in the riddle of J. Randolph Wong. He walked away deliberately and forced himself to watch some garlanded girls singing and dancing around a tall ash tree, its lower boughs festive with red plastic flowers.

A weight in his right hand made him realize: in his panic, he had run off with a bowie knife. Self-conscious, he stared at it for a moment, then slid it under his belt, feeling like a buccaneer.

"Yggdrasil," Julian murmured, coming up behind him. "Yggdrasil, the sacred ash." His voice was relaxed. He seemed to have lost the urgency of his search. They dallied at some of the exhibits and stopped in at "Tossing the Bomb," where Frank's natural talents emerged, bearing remorse like a gift. There were impact-grenades in the shape of baseballs, and spread out beyond the bunkers, a broad, badly scarred landscape map of the world: bomb the capital of your choice. Vaporize three in a row, win a Saturday-night special. Frank led off, lobbing one into Moscow, raising the familiar mushroom.

Julian, no athlete, hit Belgrade, more or less by accident. Not the first time in history, he observed.

Baseball? Frank's father had sneered. *Baseball finds work for idle hands.*

Frank zipped one, sizzling, into Mexico City: the long, terrifying roar, bodies frying in fire storms. He felt again that old kinesthetic frenzy, the killer instinct.

Baseball is a cop-out, a pop-up, an intentional walk. At thirty, you'll be a broken bat.

Frank knuckled a grenade at Peking, and missed, high and outside. Why, on that one ultimately meaningless matter, had he chosen to defeat his father? Little League, corrupter of youth; high school varsity, seducer of teenagers; college ball; the minors. Why had it meant so much, that fatal instinct?

It was all in the muscles. Control was his true gift. Frank toed the mound, blazed one into Delhi: that last bitter argument, the final separation, the symbolic beanball that sent his father to the showers, terminal, *non serviam*.

"Father!" he cried aloud, watching the panorama of the past through a crimson mist. "Forgive me."

And then Berlin was rubble again.

The epicenter will not hold. He scrubbed away tears with his sleeve.

Julian had an arm around his shoulders, leading him off. "It wasn't that way, Frank. You mustn't go on brooding about it. It's been five years since your daddy died."

"He knew the shape of it all. It's no world for second stringers, he always said." Frank dug in his pocket for a handkerchief, honked his desolation. "He knew the score. It's not beanbag out there, he always said. There are no neutral umps."

"He didn't know it all. No suicide has ever known it all. By definition. Anyway, none of it was your fault, at the end. Not the foreclosures, the bankruptcy, the despair. You mustn't go on blaming yourself."

Not his fault? Then whose fault was it that bound him to the past like leg irons?

Julian pulled Frank through the door of a large stockade, a circular structure with rough pine walls, anonymous as the cockfighting tent but open to the sky. Inside, a bullring was circled by a five-foot wooden barrier. Frank was buffeted by noise, the yelping of dogs, bellowing of a beleaguered bull, the howls of spectators.

And as at the cockfight, a sheriff's deputy was discreetly keeping an eye on the illegal operation, checking the receipts.

In the ring the mastiffs were hysterical, going foolishly head-on for the throat of the fierce beast, the great black head still keeping control. Frank saw two dogs tossed, their guts trailing in sawdust. Still, the bull hadn't got off scot-free; his flanks flowed steadily with a dark red luster.

"Old-time fun," Julian muttered, "for everyone."

"Weirdest damn fair I ever saw." Frank watched incredulously as the handlers held back the dogs for a moment, while others, graceful as picadors, stabbed long-fused firecrackers into the bull's withers, and blew pepper into his nose. The bull rampaged around the ring, exploding sneezes, the banging firecrackers terrifying and enraging him. When the dogs attacked again, the bull caught one of them on a horn and jammed it against the wall so hard the boards made a splintering sound. The dog twitched and slavered in the sawdust. The crowd cheered. Feeling nauseous, Frank turned away.

At a fanfare of car horns, they went outside. A parade was coming, the visage of Big Olaf peering down at them from fluttering banners: the heavy red mustache, burning blue eyes, shaggy brows. Sheriff's Department cruisers were weaving through the midway, horns and sirens blaring. People pushed to make room, squeezing Frank and Julian against the board wall of the bullbaiting ring.

The sheriff's car, streaming red plastic ribbons, pulled to a stop nearby. The crowd cheered in unison, sounding orchestrated. Hoisted to the car top, Big Olaf began speaking into a bullhorn. Deputies made a phalanx around him. Julian squinted, nudged Frank, and wheezed in his ear, "Look at the face."

Frank stared. He might not have noticed it himself, but Julian saw everything. The face held the outline of the virile Olaf on the billboards, but there were subtle differences. The bushy red mustache was thinned out, stringy, and unnaturally orange; the hairline had receded; the lines in the cheeks were deep and uncertain; and around the eyes the tissues had broken down in a network of wavering creases. It was the face of an aged man.

Still, the voice came deep and threatening through the tinny speaker, fragments of orator's rhetoric as the bullhorn turned this way and that, and then aimed straight at them. "We're going to smash and mangle every plank in their hypocritical platform!"

Applause and shouts erupted in the midway. Julian nudged Frank. Unaccountably edgy, Frank began to applaud whenever anyone else did.

"We intend to attack them, again and once again. We intend to blast them with the weapons of truth, to rip them and tear them, till their spindly superstitions hang in shreds and tatters. And on Tuesday, *we're going to murder them at the polls!*"

One of Olaf's deputies pulled a pistol from his holster and fired into the air, and at this prompting everyone clapped and cheered frantically. *"Murder them!"* someone yelled close by, and Frank clapped halfheartedly, wishing he were back at the motel.

But Olaf's tone had altered. The bullhorn swung this way and that, and Frank heard fragments of campaign promises: ". . . commitment to four-laning our county roads . . . free parking . . . minimum speed . . ."

The applause was wild and genuine. The young people, teenagers, were buying it all, ecstatic, waving red plastic flowers, heaving back and forth in unison. At "minimum speed" there was an orgy of cheering and jostling. Olaf raised one arm in a victory signal. His bullhorn boomed and rasped, on and on: trailbikes, cabin cruisers, dune buggies, snowmobiles, inalienable rights.

Julian seemed puzzled and a little cranky. "Solstice rituals, Frank? But no, it's all wrong, these hick Hoosiers, they've botched it up."

The distant sound of drums sent a thrill through the crowd. People glanced knowingly at each other, elbowing the ribs of neighbors. Olaf obviously heard it, too, but he went on booming into the bullhorn. The drumming got louder and louder, and in a few minutes Frank could make out a plump young man in a clerical collar, bouncing along shoulder high on a large palanquin. Around him were the blue uniforms of the Veterans Legion and the Women's Auxiliary, an azure, bobbing sea. FATHER MAGNUS FOR SHERIFF proclaimed one long blue banner. THE HOLY MOTHER CHURCH waved another.

Magnus was speaking before his bearers came to a stop, fifty yards away, the nasal squeal of his bullhorn mocking Olaf's stentorian tones. At that distance, Frank could hear only snatches of Magnus's speech, an appeal to follow the church militant, the church of a thousand years of order.

Older people greeted his soprano phrases with hoarse cries of affirmation: "Fa-ther Mag-nus! Fa-ther Mag-nus! Fa-ther Mag-nus!"

Big Olaf turned up his volume against this competition.

There was a gradual sifting-out of people, the younger ones slipping over toward Olaf, the older toward Magnus. Frank and Julian, their backs to the bull ring wall, found themselves in Olaf's crowd. His deep voice was hammering away now—R.V.'s, big bikes, the four-car family, American pride of ownership—and the kids were waving the red flowers and cheering at every word, their blond hair bouncing rhythmically.

Magnus's followers were pressing in on their squealing hero, their hoarse yells coming at narrower intervals, frenzied. Magnus was getting less and less audible to Frank, but he heard the repeated call for a return to holy mother church, the plea to follow the sun of righteousness, to follow their devoted priest, to sacrifice, sacrifice, sacrifice. There was a jumble of phrases Frank couldn't make out, and a chorus of assent from the blue-eyed mob, a shout welling up from energies so deep that Frank could hear, wave upon wave, the howling of hairy creatures in midnight forests, the bleachers roaring in the ninth inning.

"Fa-ther Mag-nus! Fa-ther Mag-nus! Fa-ther Mag-nus!"

"What's he saying?" he yelled at Julian. But Julian didn't answer, only pulled out his notebook and ballpoint, looking studious.

The roar had apparently been not only a response but a signal. A new parade began, a snake dance, and the frenzied shouting grew to an ear-splitting howl. Big Olaf's bullhorn was drowned out in the waves of sound, his deputies obviously getting more and more nervous as the snake dance continued, all of them with their pistols drawn now, firing occasional warning shots in the air.

The mob howled in unison: *"Fa-ther Mag-nus! Fa-ther Mag-nus! Fa-ther Mag-nus!"*

Julian was moving away, squeezing through the crowd, jotting in his notebook, observing the scene like a reporter. Frank lost him in the surge of people, half stalking, half dancing around him: the sudden intolerable crush, his back grinding painfully against the rough pine wall of the bull ring, the cracking of two-by-fours, the whole wall going, the inner wall down like a domino, Frank and the closest of the crowd shoved across the boards and into the ring. Terrified, they all shrank away from the bull as the beast dug its hooves in, scraping dirt, the long horns slowly rolling.

How could the animal have singled out one victim, one specific person, in all that confusion? Shapes began to focus in the bull ring: a slight blond girl in jeans and red plaid shirt, slowly giving ground as the bull stalked her, step by step. There was a moment of near quiet, and then people began cheering again, a new game shaping up, beast and beauty. Frank stared into the circle of wild eyes, the shapeless mouths screaming for blood. Where was Julian? Where were the deputies? Why didn't they do something? The rhythmic blood-chant swelled; the mastiffs were cowering at one side of the ring; the girl slipped away to the far wall. The bull was pawing the sawdust, settling himself for the rush, his powerful haunches tense, tail switching toward the crowd, contemptuous. It was bull and girl now, ugly duel, no third parties.

But *no*, Frank felt blood pounding in his temples, a savage twitching in his thighs, wild fury in the pit of his stomach. A scream so bestial it could not have come from his own throat enveloped him as he pulled the bowie knife out of his belt, sprinted toward that black pure potency, grabbed for the nostrils, wrenched back the massive head, and, almost as if he had done it before, drove the long blade into the bull's heart.

Silence. Silence everywhere.

The animal was dead before its body would acknowledge it. Tottering on useless legs, it made slow, guttering sounds and slithered into the red sawdust. Frank's muscles quit on him. He found himself kneeling at the bull's side, smelling hot blood.

The elders took up the chant again, edging toward him on their knees. "O God our king!" the fierce whisper came. "O king our savior!"

He saw the plaid shirt moving away, gliding toward a door in the inner wall, and his legs began to carry him there, too, transporting a stranger. He heard the girl's voice, that he had heard once before. "Come. Yes, come." And now again, "Come."

But his dreamlike movements were too slow. A bony hand clamped on his wrist. He turned to stare into the face of an old man in a Legion cap, down on his knees, his eyes glowing with relentless adoration, "O God our king!" Behind him the legionnaires crept forward, their arms stretched out like a snare. In a panic he chopped at the bony hand, and it pulled away. He sprinted for the door in the wall.

There was a rumble of anger from the startled mob, a howl of pursuit, then whistles and sirens, as Olaf's deputies closed in, and a small hand bolted the door behind him, pulling him through another door in the outer wall. Already running, he felt the earth tremble under his shoes.

The small hand his only link to reality, he clutched it down the dark paths of a deserted corner of the fairgrounds, along the treacherous bottoms of mossy ravines, through a narrow stony hole, into the gloom of caverns, down dripping passages behind a tiny candle flame—"come, yes, come"—the hand steadying him through the din of waterfalls, the squealing of bats, down, down, to the perpetual silence, the gleaming limestone, rows of stalactites grim as a cage, until finally the long flight ended, the candle went out with a puff, and he was guided down—kneeling, all fours, prone—to a smooth hard place, to the silken warmth of thighs, the rush of desire—"come, yes, come"—and he came, and came, and came; and at last, to a muted sound like someone weeping, the total darkness seeped inside him.

THREE

WAS HE AWAKE? Asleep?
Alive?

Cold. He was cold: good.

Absolute darkness, absolute silence. Frank groped for some sign that a world was there, outside his head. He reached and felt nothing, whispered and got no reply, then shouted and heard echoes.

Echoes: good.

The fair. The bull. The cave. The girl. Ah, the girl. Had she been there? Had she been crying? Was it all a dream? Or was he sleeping now, dreaming he was awake? He pinched himself, hard. It hurt: good.

Make them come to you. He sat in a fetal crouch and listened, wanting the friendly blast of Hollywood mufflers, the reassuring shriek of ambulances.

Nothing, nothing.

Nothing. The beginning and the end. Dark, silent, primeval.

Fear will strike the first match: his hoarse yell banged and echoed through limestone passages, but Frank no more possessed that sound than caused the savage scream that killed the bull.

Cold. He was cold.

He thought of the girl again, remembered Nancy's slim thighs, and felt a tremor of remorse. Somewhere on the Upper West Side, Nancy was suffering his neglect, abandoned to the narcissism of her body-building husband and the rooms of full-length mirrors overlooking Central Park; and somewhere in Central Park, his teammates, the Galloping Ghostwriters, were cursing his betrayal, desperate for his shrewd pitching and his killer instinct, and getting murdered by a pickup squad from the theater district; and somewhere in the theater district, two center-aisle seats at opening night were conspicuously vacant; and somewhere in the Greatest City in the World, aproned men with middle-European accents were waiting at the deli for his sandwich order; and meticulous librarians were breathing anxiety for his overdue books; and pubescent girls in perky tutus were depending on his appearance at the annual benefit; and doctoral candidates, skirting despair, were mailing reply coupons to Confidential Services, Inc. and getting no answers; and somewhere under the earth in southern Indiana, a city boy was lost in caverns of dread and guilt.

The next scream hurt his throat, and comforted him. As the flurry of sound fussed itself away, Frank thought he heard a low whistle. He went rigid.

Were his eyes open? He touched his eyelids, stared into nothing, rotated his head consciously, owl-like, heard neck muscles grinding, incredibly loud.

A needle of light focused the blackness. Frank stared at the light, paralyzed. He thought he heard his name, rippling with echoes.

Fear will strike the first match; guilt will cast the first stone. The memory of Jessie Bell, sexual bandit of the ninth grade, mocked him down a labyrinth of years.

Will-o'-the-wisp, the little light bounced and jiggled, seemed to come closer.

It was a candle. Shadows quivered around him. Frank stood up, fighting for balance, saw the ghosts of gray stalagmites, stony forest, and saw at last behind the candle that innocent, seductive frown, coming toward him. A leaping of blood retrieved the universe. He shivered violently, closed his eyes a moment, and then she was beside him, putting a wicker basket down beside a big stalagmite, setting the candle on the basket, and snuggling into his chest, the slender arms wrapping his waist in a tight embrace. Frank gasped, hugged back, held the blond head in both hands, kissed, and reached for the small, firm breasts.

She pushed him away. "Not so fast, stranger."

"Stranger?" Frank was astonished. "But before . . ."

"Well, that was before, and you'd saved my life, you don't think I'd just . . . Anyway, now I've saved yours, so we're beginning all over again. Square one." Her fingers stroked the big stalagmite.

Frank stared at the unconscious caress, and felt a twinge of jealousy.

Saved? My life?

Then she sat down quickly by the candle. Reluctantly, bewildered, Frank sat down, too. She took a sandwich from the basket and gave it to him. He looked at it without appetite, bit into ham, and was immediately ravenous. He gobbled the sandwich. She ate one herself, handed him a plastic glass.

Wine: dry, cool. He gulped it down. For some unmeasured period, Frank ate with total concentration. A dill pickle. A deviled egg. A crisp chicken thigh. A cherry tomato. More wine. And the thought struck him: how long had he been here?

"All night. I had to go up there, to all that, because they needed me, I had work to do." She sighed. "So much to do. Saving the world is no part-time job, you know, unless you just happen to be God."

Frank smiled at her little joke, but she wasn't laughing. Her eyes were fixed on a cascade of stalactites, great soundless rippling of cavern music. "You'll never guess what those idiots are up to now," she said, anger edging into her voice. "Oh, you're such bastards, you men!"

Frank stopped eating. "Hey, what did I do?"

"I know, I know, you just got here, you're not responsible."

But faced with her indignation, Frank felt uneasy.

"Look, it's that—well, you can't get away from the blight any more, that's all, you can't escape. Except here. Only down here, deep in the earth, is there any place for . . ." She put a hand on his forehead; her warmth went through his body like a current. He reached for her again, but she stopped him.

"Things are quieter up there now, the sun . . ." She looked at Frank again with that ambiguous sideways glance—shy, or cunning—then got up, businesslike. "The sun's shining. You're rested. We have to go." She picked up the candle.

"Wait. Go where?"

"Trust me."

"But what . . ." He felt the absurdity of the question. "What's your name?"

"Frieda. It's Frieda, Frank."

"You know my name."

"Julian told me."

"Oh. You've seen him, then? You're taking me to Julian?"

"Of course." There was the slightest pause. "In a way."

What was it all about? Why the mystery? What was she up to?

"You know what, Frieda? I mean, I'm no connoisseur of midwestern towns, but what I think is—no offense, now—what I think is, I've ended up in a pretty peculiar little place."

But she only handed him the basket and picked up the candle. Sighing, he followed as she led him off, the candle pulling him along like a moth, out of the spacious cave, down long limestone corridors, past the echoing sounds of rushing water, until, in that wilderness of underground passages, Frank saw a stunningly improbable thing: a door. In the damp stone wall, a green metal door, rusty at the edges. Frank stared at it, unbelieving, but Frieda hardly paused, opened it with a key and pulled him through, clanging it shut behind them.

They were on a narrow stairway, cut into the stone. Frieda started up, and Frank trailed her, watching fascinated, in the shadow of the candle, the slow working of her thighs, that slightly off-balance, almost awkward movement, seductive as an Oriental dance.

Another unmeasured experience: a hundred steps? A thousand? They passed another door at the side of the stairs. Frank reached for the handle, but she stopped him.

"No. Not there."

They climbed again, the slender, undulating thighs at eye level obliterating time and space, until the stairway seemed not so much to end as to evolve, to level off and become a corridor again, but this time less a cave than a basement, quarried rock walls that vaulted overhead in a long tunnel. The candle revealed no end to it.

Frieda walked briskly, as if on familiar terrain. The tunnel made a turn, then another. They were climbing slightly, still climbing. How deep in the earth had they been, Frank wondered.

"Where in the world are we?" His voice was hollow, echoing. "What is this thing? Who built it?"

She shrugged, impatient. "Ash Garden is old, Frank. Very old."

"What do you mean, 'old'? Old like New York? London? Rome? They were hunting with bows and arrows out here not long ago."

But she wouldn't answer, didn't look back, and even as he said it, he felt foolish. Those walls. Megaliths.

"This way." The tunnel kept branching out, other tunnels leading off to left and right, a maze. At last another door. Frieda led Frank through it, shushed him with a finger to her lips, then led him up a tight circular staircase, at the end of which she blew out her candle. They crawled on hands and knees for a few yards, then eased up, still kneeling, and peered cautiously over a stone railing.

From the aerial perspective of the narrow balcony, Frank stared at the strange gathering: men and women knelt along the walls of a dim twelve-sided room, in the smoky light of a dozen torches. At the far side, before a flaming altar, stood Father Magnus in midnight-blue robes, his arms raised in a triumphant V. A blue banner floated above the altar: THE HOLY MOTHER CHURCH.

Frank looked at Frieda, surprised. She frowned at him.

Some sort of service was in progress. Magnus was intoning, "*Gloria in excelsis Deo*. I invoke the Lord of high pastures. I invoke the sun himself, most glorious word incarnate." He wiped his fingers daintily on a small cloth. "O sun of our lives, O mediator, let the bull of our springtime coming and the scorpion of our autumn going tell our souls' salvation."

Odd kind of prayer, Frank thought. Like everything else around here.

"We remember, O mediator, the stars that shone in the twelve holy houses, the favorable trines and sextiles, the wind in the trees, the very earth beneath our feet divine."

"What's all this about?" Frank whispered. Frieda shook her head sternly and shushed him.

"Just listen."

"But this day, O holiest, the unbelievers have muddied the stream of thy truth, and mother earth sickens in their Godless pollution. Grant us, thy servants, salvation from the forces of darkness."

Frieda edged closer to him. "Did you hear, Frank? You understand?" Her arm slid around his waist; he felt a trap closing on him.

"And now in the deep of the solstice, let us speak in tongues and with the gift of prophecy."

Bleating sounds rose from the kneeling worshipers. Magnus's voice whinnied above them.

"O powerful, we see in a glass, darkly, two forces contending for life. And the forces of light . . ." Magnus paused, his eyes lifted. Then his pudgy face brightened and his voice rang with triumph, "The forces of light shall be the elect! And the forces of darkness will be crushed!"

Ecstasy squealed and brayed in the congregation, and Frieda shivered, her hug sending tremors through Frank's body.

"And the cry of death shall rule the land, and the sea will rise up, and the minions of darkness will perish."

"What's he saying?" Frank whispered.

"They always speak in tongues and prophesy in the season of the solstice. They always know, at midsummer. Father Magnus will win. There'll be death, and the sea—the sea will rise up."

"Wait a minute! Start over. Back up. What's the solstice got to do with this? What . . ."

"Shhh." Her face was a mask of severity. He was getting too loud. "Listen. That's why I brought you here. You must listen and understand." Her whisper got softer; he strained to hear it. "It's nearly Midsummer Day. They say that once the birds sang a prophecy on this day, and they say that at dawn the sun would shine toward the altar at . . ."

She stopped. Was it doubt there, in her curious sideways glance? Guile? "Go on," he whispered.

But she sat motionless, looking down.

"And what about that 'sea' stuff? This is the Midwest, for God's sake."

"Just wait. They're never wrong. It will be after the election, and the losers . . ."

She wouldn't go on. A strange, strange girl. Frank guessed at motives: piety? insanity? What was she up to? What's in it for her?

He glanced down at the crowd. The congregation was on its feet, all speaking in tongues, a babble. Tall, mostly blond and blue-eyed, they were a handsome people, in a way, but sinister—something smug about their stance, self-righteous. The blue uniforms of the Veterans Legion and the Women's Auxiliary were everywhere.

"I know you better than you think." She smiled, as if forgiving him all his sins. It occurred to him: he hadn't seen her smile before. "You're an Aquarius, aren't you?"

Frank was startled, and wary. How did she know? He shrugged. "For what it's worth."

She was shining, all her gravity gone. "I knew it. I'm Cancer, my birthday's next Tuesday, I'll be eighteen. We're air and water, our conjunctions will be right, you'll see!"

Oh, God, she's only seventeen years old? Jailbait?

But she kissed him impulsively, like a child, then passionately, and Frank forgot about her tender years and her little mysteries, and only half heard the service proceeding, prayer by prayer.

Sitting back, they stared at each other, marveling. What was it about her? It made him dizzy to look into her eyes, as if, all at once, anything was possible. Seventeen or not, with her, anything, anything at all, was suddenly possible. He reached for her hand again. Fingers touched; electric circuits jangled all over his body. She was as quiet now as if she'd been cut from cavern stone.

But what's wrong with her? Why is she so strange?

Holding her hands, something came to him. It wasn't like holding a woman's hands at all, it was . . . He pulled them up close to his face. They were calloused and cracked, the hands of a mechanic, ground-in dirt around the nails. She pulled them away from him and held them behind her.

"You must understand," she whispered, as if answering a question.

They sat quietly, through yet another gap in the ordered universe, and against his will he was slipping into the wells of those blue eyes and falling, falling, through some medium that was not quite air, not quite water, slow motion head-over-heels in a bottomless shaft of blue. When did it begin, when will it end? Why ask? Silly. Irrelevant. He jests at scars, that never felt a wound.

She had said something.

"What?"

"There's a little more sermon you should hear, and then we'll have to go. Fast."

They watched again. Magnus was getting worked up, the rhythm of his nasal soprano building to periodic climaxes. He could speak just as well breathing in as breathing out, so he never had to slow down or pause. "My brothers and sisters in glory, we have borne witness to the second coming. He walks among us, even this very day, in our streets, he watches over us. Pray that he join us in this great crusade, and tomorrow, led by the ever constant stars, we shall sweep away the heathen, and once again our heavenly order will rule for a thousand years."

"You understand?" she whispered.

No. No, he certainly did not.

To the rhythm of Magnus's exhortations, a black bull was being led down the central aisle. He was not hobbled or tied, but was led docile by young girls in gauzy dresses. They were stroking his garlanded neck, his ribs, his flank.

And Fat Mama herself, stately in flowing white robes, was stroking his belly. Frank stared. The great pizzle was fully extended, lolling regally.

Magnus was ecstatic, and the worshipers murmured their approval. Frieda tugged at him. "OK, you've heard it. Now we've got to get out of here."

"Out?" Frank was astonished. "Now?"

"We've got to go while we still can. You've heard what you needed to hear."

Her appeal could have sent Frank leaping through beds of crimson coals, but now he was snarled in Magnus's puzzle. He couldn't leave. He half stood, getting a better look at the bizarre procession. Frieda gasped and pulled him back down.

"You can't!" she whispered, frantic. "They mustn't see you!" She tried to get him to the door, but Frank wouldn't be dragged away now. He clutched the railing and kept on watching. The bull was nearly to the altar. Magnus's round face was a wash of pious joy. "Hail to thee, holy bull! Hail to thee who makest increase!"

As if by signal, pregnant women from the congregation slipped out of their places and paraded slowly to the altar. They gathered there, all degrees of fullness.

The bull was at the altar now, and the young girls were making washing gestures, as if cleansing him. Fat Mama continued to stroke his belly and occasionally the pizzle itself, which trembled at her touch. The bull stood passive, as if drugged.

"Damn it, we have to get out of here."

What was she trying to hide from him? "I've got to see the rest of it."

"This is my body," Magnus intoned, and performed the ensuing ritual in a way Frank found disturbingly familiar: the elevation of the long blade, the grasp at the unsuspecting nostrils, the wrenching back of the head, the terrible thrust to the heart. The bull slid down on the altar.

Magnus withdrew the blade and elevated it, dripping, then put it to his tongue. "And this is my blood." He smacked his lips. "Welcome, fecundity, welcome to the banquet of life."

The pregnant women filed by the carcass, each one dipping a finger into the oozing wine and touching it to her lips. The young girls followed, then the whole congregation. Some of the women pulled up their skirts and crossed their stomachs with the blood. Fat Mama was at the altar. Even from high in the balcony she was an impressive sight, tall, majestic, severe. The pregnant women were all on their knees at her feet, and she was blessing them with signs, her fingers crimson. Then, one by one, they began to file out of the room.

Frank sat there, dazed. Frieda had moved away from him, scowling. "It's too late now."

Frank looked up and shook his head sharply. "Too late for what?"

"They're all out there, at the doors, in the street. How will I get you away? Voyeur!" She hissed her contempt like a cat: "Tourist!" Her ferocity bewildered him. "You call yourself an Aquarius? You're just like the others, you're like a—a Pisces! I should let them take you, crown you hero, like Lucky—and you, lucky you, could be king for a day, and have your pick of all our girls, and end by knowing the mystery of mysteries! Men, oh God, men!"

(Schtoonk! Jessie shrieked at him. Schlemiel!)

In her fury, Frieda glowed with a poisonous beauty. Her contempt blistered him. "Lucky?" he ventured.

"Lucky, yes, Lucky. Down there in the cave."

"Frieda, wait a minute. What are you talking about? What cave?"

Trembling with anger, she tilted her head. Tears yawed across her cheeks. "It's for the men, of course, always the men. And for God. That's why he's there, it's his luck, his fate, his glory."

No use. She was beyond him. Frank felt the hostile seconds creeping by. "Frieda." He touched her arm. "Let's go. Out of this loony place. They've all gone now. We can make it. Can't we?"

She sat there in a springing of tears, her anger blown out. "But it will be dangerous. It would have been simple before. The risk . . ."

She paused, then wiped her eyes and began foraging in her wicker basket, all business. "Here. Wear these. I brought them in case of trouble, and now we have it. They were my father's, my runaway father, that slippery Pisces who came and went like a March wind, before I was born. Men!"

Frank took off his shoes and put on the ones she gave him, old-fashioned wing tips, three sizes too big. She wrapped up his own shoes and slipped them into the basket.

At the outside door she paused, and they peeked out cautiously. A parade of horsemen came by, the leader flying Magnus's blue banner, the blue campaign caps of the Legion bobbing and rippling along the street. Frieda quickly eased the door shut, leaving only a crack. "The hunt," she whispered.

No sooner had they gone by than another group passed, young men and women on roaring Hondas and Kawasakis. There was an air of holiday, but the rifles of Magnus's veterans were serious enough.

In spite of a sudden eddying of fear, Frank found the whole thing silly. Nervous laughter rose in his chest, bubbled over. He tapped Frieda on the shoulder. "What are they all after, anyway?"

She stared at him. "But I thought you understood, Frank." She paused, as if embarrassed. Looking up at him, the blue eyes were reproachful.

"You, my simple Aquarius. They're all after you."

FOUR

OWNHILL all the way: bustling Sunday crowds at the shopping centers, an occasional siren shrilling in the distance. In front of their limestone houses, people were washing Cougars and Bobcats, Firebirds and Skyhawks, Crickets and Beetles, rubbing wax into hoods. Bumper stickers glowed on every car.

GUNS DON'T KILL PEOPLE
PEOPLE KILL PEOPLE

Frank held on to the wicker basket and to Frieda's rough hand, feeling homesick. It was the sirens that did it, the sirens of New York, once learned in the blood, never forgotten; also the constant graffiti—SAVE SUNRISE PARK—spray-painted on walls, some of them hasty and crude, others four-color creations, stylized and fancy, evoking nostalgia for the subways.

The distant baying of hounds had been charming—rural, antebellum. But it was getting louder and louder, and soon it was clear that the hunt was returning, coming up the street toward them. Little tweezers of dread picked at Frank's guts. *They're all after you.*

Frieda was glancing about nervously, her small grip tight on his hand. "Over here, Frank!" She steered him through window shoppers toward a department store and pointed to jeans and skirts like an insistent Sunday wife. The baying was directly behind them now. In the window Frank watched the reflected stallions, banners, blue campaign caps, rifles. He fought against the bitterness in his throat. High-pitched yips from the hunters kept the bloodhounds in a constant froth of excitement. Frank squeezed his eyes closed and braced himself for the charge, the canine teeth ripping his thighs.

But no, it wasn't happening. He opened his eyes. The dogs were all loping on by, snuffling their way uphill. Frank felt his legs go rubbery.

It wasn't over yet. Riding with the hunters, astride a frisky mare, was a lean man in a snap-brim, his beady eyes darting right to left, left to right. Frank stopped breathing.

Then he passed by, too, and all the others. It took a long time for the whole baying, howling procession to file past. Frank realized he was leaning on Frieda like an invalid. "Your father's old oxfords worked." He tried to smile.

She kissed him, then broke away quickly, easing his hands off her hips, holding them clasped in her own, a four-handed prayer. "They mustn't catch you."

"I don't even know why they want me."

"They fear you. Olaf fears you. Magnus needs you." Her voice broke and she looked down quickly. Frank stared at her, immediately suspicious.

"But why?"

Her mouth was puckered, sober. She spoke gravely, like an oracle. "Magnus wants you to be God." She peered up at him shyly. "I want you to be mine." She said it as if reciting a formula. "I am to teach you how to love."

Frank tensed up again: that archaic flatness, the irritating mystery. God? How to love? He felt like a lamb being chosen for the altar. Somewhere hounds were baying. His bewilderment mounted to anger. "Frieda, you've got to tell me, damn it! What am I getting into here? What does this crazy town want from me? What do *you* want?"

Holding his hand, she led him down the sidewalk again. "I'll try."

But a hundred yards went pacing uphill behind them, before she began. She was having trouble with her voice, opening her mouth to speak and making no sound. "Once upon a time," she finally said.

Frank sighed. She was reciting again.

"Once upon a time, in a country of hills and caves, everyone lived in fear of the savage trolls who constantly ravaged the land. Leading the fierce bull, Armin, and a venomous plague of scorpions, the trolls slaughtered the brave people who stood and fought them, and carried off prisoners to their endless caverns. Everyone lived in fear, then, of the terrible raids, knowing that after the last bloodshed, the stars that guide our destinies would flicker out, and the land would freeze in a long, black winter.

"The people prayed to the Lord, who at last heard their supplication and caused a miracle. His lightning struck a stone, and out of the cleft in that rock the shepherds saw a holy man emerge, a friar, carrying a sword and a lighted torch, and accompanied by a faithful dog."

Bloodhounds somewhere nearby sent their quivering music through Frank's nerves.

"The torch was so bright it lighted the darkness of the interminable winter, and the friar demanded of the quaking shepherds why he had been called out of the stone.

"'O friar,' they said, 'the trolls and scorpions and the black bull, Armin, have laid waste our land, and we have prayed to the Lord of Heaven to shelter us.'

"The friar's torch burned brighter, and he commanded, 'Bring me your warriors.' And when they came and looked on the friar's sword and flaming torch, they were filled with courage, and followed him into battle.

"The fray was brief and bloody. The friar soon sank his gleaming sword in the heart of the black bull, Armin, and his faithful hound routed the scorpions, and the warriors scattered the trolls.

"And then the world was changed, for out of the body of the dying bull sprang up the wheat that makes our bread, and from his blood the vine that charms our wines. And the guiding stars moved through the heavens once more, and the torch of the friar burned fiercely, warming the long, black winters. But the friar himself went back into the stone from which he appeared, and lives today in the vastness of the central cave, and will come again to help us when our need is great."

Her voice had lowered to a whisper. Frank looked at her, expecting a smile of self-mockery; but she kept her face straight ahead, solemn.

"That was an explanation?" he asked gently.

The severity came back, her voice sharp with anger. "You must understand, Frank."

"I'm supposed to understand that crazy story?"

She frowned. "Not crazy, Frank, just unfinished."

What was it about her? That slim young innocence, maddening enigma. Was she just playing coy games? Or was it all some kind of elaborate trap?

But every move she made was so artless, nature's own simplicity. The way she carried her hands—open, loose, palms slightly forward.

And she sounded earnest. "Some day, it is said, the stars will send us this miracle again, and the friar will appear on earth, and the tale will be ended at last. Don't you see?"

His confusion was obviously irritating her. The anger bristled in her voice. "Mama will help you. God!"

Rage, Frank thought. She functions on rage.

They were at the Steak and Lobster again; but at the back door, where instead of neon, a weathered shingle displayed the two crudely drawn animals, burned into wood.

From here Frank could see that the shiny motel was a false front, a later addition. The main building was an old limestone structure, rambling and dilapidated. They went inside.

Wassail merriment pealed from the dining room. Frieda guided him past the closed doors, down a long hall to her own room, where they sat quietly for a moment, facing each other. Frank looked down at his oversized shoes and felt like a clown.

"Where's Julian?" he asked.

"Probably at the smorgasbord."

"Should we go in?"

She looked disappointed. "You really don't understand?"

His frustration boiled over. "No, by God, so far I don't understand one damn thing! And whose fault is that?" He forced himself to stop, literally biting his lip.

She clenched her fists but said nothing, obviously struggling to keep her temper. When she permitted herself to speak, she was surprisingly patient. "It's because they're in here, too. Some of them are out in the streets, but some always come here right after services, and drink. A lot. Wait a minute." She held a finger up to his lips, then moved her hand over his cheek. "I think I can find you a suitable face." She slipped out of the room.

Frank wasn't exactly tired, but he was too weary in spirit to stop her with more questions. He sat and stared at the bed, her bed. He thought of Nancy's saffron sheets, and fantasies began to slip across his drowsy consciousness, Nancy's lovely breasts, Frieda's welcoming thighs; but as he felt the arousal, he remembered Jessie Bell and her terrible hammerlock, and her strong hands pulling off his pants . . .

He was glad when Frieda slipped back into the room, as silently as she had left, carrying a cardboard box. He put an arm around her and pulled her to the bed. Graceful, wiry, she eased out of his grasp.

"Not now."

Hunger choked him. "When, then?"

She gave him that innocent, grave look: "Later. Afterwards."

He almost queried her—after what?—but stopped himself. He hadn't had a straight answer yet. Anyway, it was a promise. Or sounded like a promise.

She was taking things out of the box—beards, mustaches. "From our Sunday School pageants, one for every disciple. Here's Saint Thomas, auburn-haired like you. Try it on, it'll make you a whole new person. Give you a new life."

"Who wants to be a new person?" he protested. "I liked my old life fine."

"Would you rather go into hiding?" The edge came into her voice again.

"Wait a minute. I haven't done anything, why should I have to . . ."

"Everybody's done something. Now hold still. You're about to be reborn." She seated him in a chair and opened a bottle of sharp-smelling liquid.

Once he saw it in the mirror, he didn't really mind the mustache. Full and slightly droopy, it lent his features a maturity he'd always felt missing. But Frieda wasn't finished; the reddish beard reached his breastbone and was touched with gray. He gasped when he saw it. His father rose up and glared from the mirror.

"There now, you're a new man." She got up to leave. "Come in the dining room after me, alone, as if you were just staying here in the motel. Mama will probably know you, but I don't think anyone else will."

She stopped at the door. "Oh, what's your new name, your alias? Choose."

"With this big red bush?" He considered it: play along, humor her. "Something Scandinavian. How about Leif Ericson?"

"Commonplace," she sniffed. "You deserve something more original. Like Heimdall. Or Balder. Or Freyr. Yes, Freyr will do very nicely. I'll see you in the dining room, Mr. Freyr."

When she was gone, Frank gazed into the mirror, confronting that somber, paternal mask. An alias, God, what next? This whole small-town charade was so ludicrous he had to snicker. "The bull of our springtime coming! Lucky! Trolls! Scorpions!" When he finally stopped laughing, he felt the tears on his face. The mirror image stared back at him with contempt. "Freyr!" he snorted.

But he proceeded to the dining room with a deliberate step. God-like.

FIVE

IT WAS NOT an orderly scene. The long plank tables were crowded with food, strange-looking dishes Frank didn't recognize, and flagons of wine. At one end of the hall, a tipsy quartet in Legion uniforms was blending bawdy lyrics to the tune of "Back Home Again in Indiana."

And the lamb shall lie down with lions. Frieda was at one of the tables, filling a plate. Avoid her.

Mastering his nervousness, he made his way through the crowd, inspecting the tables. The centerpiece of one was a big tray of lobsters on chipped ice. A dozen blue-skirted auxiliaries and potbellied legionnaires wearing six-guns and paper bibs sat around the table, devouring succulent morsels with messy gusto. But most of them were at the steak bar, where a white-capped cook bustled around a grill full of sizzling T-bones.

Where was Julian?

It was some minutes before he saw him, standing in a smoky corner with Fat Mama, gesturing as he talked. Frank edged over to them. When Fat Mama saw him approaching, she winked, and her huge frame shook a little. "Hi, there, come join us. Have a bowl of mead, specialty of the house." She poured him one.

Julian glanced at him briefly, then looked away, and at that motion of annoyance, Frank knew his disguise was going to work. Julian hated irrelevancies.

"Julian, meet Mr.—uh, what was it again?"

"Freyr. I'm down in number eight."

At the sound of his voice, Julian's head jerked around. "What was that name again?"

"Mr. Freyr. Just call me Frank."

"Such a coincidence," Fat Mama bubbled. "Taurus here was just talking about Thor and Odin and all those graybearded farts." She walked away, laughing.

"And Freyr. Sun-god. God of fertility. I was talking about Freyr." Julian's irritation was growing. Like most intellectuals, he was impatient with coincidence. He pulled Frank aside. "Why Freyr?" he croaked, barely audible.

Frank whispered back: "Why anything? Why me? And where the hell were you when I needed you?" He felt his new dignity slipping away.

Julian looked uncomfortable. "I knew you were safe. Sybil told me." His right eyebrow clenched as if holding a monocle. "I've been learning things here. A lot of things."

Things? The image of J. Randolph Wong hovered between them, scouring Frank's nerves. "Me, too, Julian. Learning one hell of a lot. In fact, I've learned enough to jump right in that Stingray out there and get the hell back to New York where I belong, before those goddam bloodhounds get at my jugular."

Julian was hardly listening, getting more and more excited. Frank knew the mood. Before long he'd be gorging himself and lecturing nonstop. Julian pulled him farther aside. "Don't let these country bumpkins get to you, with their dogs and their guns. They're just a bunch of hillbillies who think they're extras in a B movie, obviously harmless. Anyway, we're on to the Vikings at last, nipping at their heels. And something else besides, something incredible. Tell me, where were they hiding you?"

"In a cave."

"A cave? Perfect! Where is it? What's it like?" He pulled Frank farther aside, away from the noisy legionnaires.

Frank shrugged. "You've seen one cave, you've seen 'em all."

But he described Magnus's service, and Fat Mama's impressive role in it, and Frieda's story of Armin and the friar. Julian's little eyes went round as pennies.

Fat Mama's throaty laugh played over them. She was nearby, bantering with the hunters. "Did you hear the one about the traveling Taurus and the farmer's Virgo?"

Julian drank from his mead bowl. "Listen, this goes way beyond Wong, but somehow he's involved, and Sybil knows all about it. She knows all about everything. Leading a bull to sacrifice, was she? Fantastic!"

Sure enough, Julian was edging toward the food tables.

"I don't care if she's the *Encyclopaedia Britannica*. This place is unhealthy for me, and I'm getting out while I'm still wearing my own accelerator foot. Julian, think of the business we're losing, twenty thousand a month shot to hell, it's obscene."

"Tush, boy, money isn't everything." Julian had reached the table. "Have a canape." He was munching on something unidentifiable. "Mmm. Try this."

"Julian, I'm serious. Are you coming with me, or do I go alone?" Frank grabbed a flagon and poured himself another bowl of mead.

"So am I serious, as serious as I've ever been in my life. More so." Julian's voice lowered. "Frank, there's a lot more to this little place than meets an untutored eye. What we've got to do . . ." He looked around furtively, then whispered, "What we've got to do is get back to that cave."

Fat Mama moved in on them again, her low-pitched laugh rippling the magnificent cleavage. "You fellows doing all right over here?"

"I'm fine, Sybil, never been better. But Frank is a bit jumpy."

Fat Mama winked at him. "Scared? Listen, it's all right, Mr. Freyr. We'll take care of you. It's a good week for Geminis."

Frank shifted and looked away. He'd forgotten that she thought he was a Gemini, and that he'd misled her. Not that it really mattered. So why did he feel uneasy about it?

"Have confidence in those with greater experience," she went on.

"Aim at increasing rapport. Be wary of those who only pretend friendship."

"OK, OK," Frank protested. He lowered his voice. "But who do you think all these clowns with the elephant guns are after? Guess."

Fat Mama hovered over a platter of something that resembled a stuffed udder, and with a gleaming double-edged knife sliced off two of the nipples. "You'll be safe here, Gemini. Try these, boys, the best part."

Julian gobbled his tidbit like an underfed shark, but Frank stood there holding the thing at arm's length, feeling silly. He couldn't bring himself to eat it.

"Mmm," Julian murmured. But then, he always did that.

Frank had to ask, "What's this?"

"Shit, Red, it's not going to bite you." Fat Mama elbowed him. "What's it look like? Go ahead, eat it. Enjoy!"

Frank was embarrassed. He put the slippery thing in his mouth. Chewed. It was delicious. "Mmm."

Fat Mama laughed. The sound was a river of honey rippling on golden pebbles. She moved closer to Frank, her bare cleavage slowly moving with her laugh. Frank gulped the mead.

She took his arm. Her skin was much warmer than his. "You see, Mr. Freyr, you can trust Fat Mama." Sun-god? God of fertility? When she touched his arm, Frank had an instant erection. He was ashamed of himself. She was old enough to be his . . .

"Sow's udders always do it." Fat Mama smirked. "For sheer getting it up, they're better than powdered rhinoceros horn, better than crushed cantharis or ginseng tea or mandrake root." Julian leaned closer, listening intently. "Better than prairie oysters or lion's fat or bat's blood. Or dried salamander or camel's hump. Or raw eels."

Julian was slicing off another nipple and straining to hear the hypnotic voice. Fat Mama filled Frank's bowl. His erection would not relent, and he thought again of Jessie Bell—predatory, treacherous, promiscuous at fourteen—why did her sullen Bronx image keep coming to him here in this little midwestern town? Schlump! her nasal voice dinged at him, schmuck!

Julian moved closer. "Sybil," he breathed, his lips curling, the portrait of a Roman voluptuary, "help me." He slurped an oyster off its half-shell and offered one to her.

Fat Mama swallowed it, sidled up to him, rubbed her haunch along his. Julian's left hand reached out and fondled the ripe buttocks. Frank began to get queasy. "Help me, Sybil, I need you," Julian was crooning, shifting slowly on the balls of his feet like some implausible dancer.

Fat Mama was moving with him, her lovely eyes rolling with anticipation. "Yes, Julian, baby, my terrific tantalizing Taurus."

"Tell me," he murmured, his voice low and confidential. "Tell me about Magnus and that bull you were leading. Tell me about J. Randolph Wong."

Her laughter suffused through the room, shaped the motley banquet noises, slipped through windows and doors, and focused the limestone countryside. "Oh, Julian, you precious, preposterous son of a bitch!" Flesh quivered all over her body.

Julian was unabashed, his right hand steadily delivering stuffed figs first to his own mouth, then teasingly to Fat Mama's, his left hand cupping her buttocks in spasms of desire.

"You know," Julian insisted. "You know it all. Please, Sybil."

Her merriment was infectious. Frank grinned at Julian, relaxed a little. Turning her back to the legionnaires, she pulled at a fine golden chain around her neck. Slowly, from the depths of that rosy cleavage, a gold locket emerged. Frank imagined it warm from its resting place.

She dangled it at Julian, swinging like a pendulum. Julian's eyes followed it intently: a hypnotist's jewel, the tawny gold of Mycenae, of Scythia. He reached out and palmed it, turned it over. Frank looked over his shoulder. The fine patina was scratched with writing.

Frank recognized the symbols—runes, like the parchments of J. Randolph Wong. Julian was transfixed. He fondled the locket, brought it closer to his trifocals. His voice was a gasp. "Where did you get it?"

"Curiosity, Taurus, killed the pussycat."

"Sybil, God damn it, the truth for a change."

Fat Mama suddenly stiffened, her smile gone, and Frank remembered the haughty Sybil at Magnus's bloody rites. He glanced from her to Julian, from Julian to her. They were glaring at each other as if in combat. Frank half expected them to paw the floor.

"Why," she said, her voice brittle, "I got it from my mother. And she from her mother. And . . ."

"I see." Julian looked as if he'd been kicked. He dropped the locket abruptly. It dangled on the great bosom for a moment, then she slipped it back inside her blouse. Julian was indignant. When he spoke again, it was stiffly, with an air of one-last-chance. "Sybil. Will you help me with Wong?"

The din of the banqueting was oppressive. She relented, but grudgingly. "Maybe. If you earn it, tonight." She sliced off another nipple with a vicious slash of the two-edged knife, and handed it to him like a challenge. "Eat up. There may have been an envelope left for you. Ask me about it later."

She swung off toward the riotous legionnaires and auxiliaries, the broad hips forming luscious parabolas, leaving Julian agape. "Envelope!" he whispered to Frank. "More parchment from Wong? It's got to be. Frank, he knows we're here!" Julian was seething with excitement and frustration. He shuffled off to the table of T-bones.

Frank was depressed. Julian obviously wouldn't leave town now. And *he* couldn't stay. But could he go back to New York without Julian? What would he do for moral support? Therapy? Friendship? A living? Trying to get along without Julian would be—what would it be? He thought of his father's old precepts: *Don't get it right, get it written. Second place is for widows and kids. Success speaks louder than sermons, failure speaks louder than alibis.* He felt warm all over, for a moment, then more depressed than ever.

Frieda touched his arm. "Well, Aquarius, what did Mama tell you?"

Frank laughed bitterly. "Mama told me I'm a Gemini." She looked so startled that Frank took pity and changed the subject. "She showed us her locket."

Frieda smiled. "It'll be mine some day." She was a beaming little girl, proud of her trinkets.

On an impulse, Frank caught her wrist and looked closely at her bracelets: tawny gold, a fine patina, and on one of them, a thick, solid one, faint runic scrawls, all the way around.

And along, under, and through the scribblings, the gliding body of a serpent.

Frank realized he was sweating. "Where did you get these?"

Could such a wistful, earnest face be betraying him? "I've always had them, Frank. Mama gave them to me when I was little. I teethed on this one, see?"

Innocence. Frank stared at the rich gold, slightly dented.

"Mama has lots of them."

"Lots? Like this?"

Her wrist worked free from his grasp, and he caught a glimpse of her chronic anger. "You're always making me feel guilty. Why do you do that?"

"*I'm* always . . ." He sputtered. "How do you think you make me feel, you and your mother." His erection returned, painful. He cursed the sow's nipples.

But she seemed determined to be cheerful. She put away anger, and her quick smile was genuine, a parable: anything, anything was possible. "Let me tell your fortune. Give me your hand."

But he was not so mercurial. He had his new dignity to think of. "Not so fast. My fortune is all I've been getting since I came here."

She poured him, and then herself, a bowl of mead. "That's not very nice to say, lover, after last night."

Those baffling switches—stranger, lover, teething, afterward. He pulled her aside where they couldn't be overheard. "Tell me now, who are all these people? What are they here for? Why aren't they home watching TV with the kiddies, or out at the fair or a ball game or something?"

"Why, because they're on a hunt. It's the most important thing, to them."

"OK, then why aren't they out there on their nags, taking their chances with the semi's, going after . . ." He stopped.

There was a slight pause.

"After you, Mr. Freyr," she prompted.

"Yeah. After me." He was bitter. "So if they're supposed to be out hunting me, how come they're sousing it up in here?"

"Sundays they're never very serious. That's why I could get you here in the first place, all the way from the church. This is traditional on Sundays, the steaks, the lobsters, the mead. Especially now, with the election coming."

"Sons of bitches and their goddam cannons." Frank was feeling grumpier every minute. He finished off the bowl with a reckless chugalug.

"You're taking it too personally, Frank."

"With all those bloodhounds out there in the street? And those .357 magnums? Too personally?"

"I mean you have to be careful, of course, but you mustn't feel offended. It's not a campaign against you, as such."

"Frieda. Look me right in the eye and tell me. What have these people got against me?"

She looked him in the eye, then glanced down. "Nothing. Nothing at all."

"But then . . ."

"It's the others who want you dead. They . . ."

"Wait a minute—dead?"

"Olaf, I mean. These people, I told you, want you to—well, they want you to be God." She sighed. "But that's almost the same thing." She looked around for a moment, to be sure no one else was listening, and when she spoke again, it was with that half-turned glance of hers, shy, or cunning. "Do you ever think of yourself as God?"

He was so astonished he could only stare.

"I mean, you don't always have to know you're a god to be one, isn't that right? Don't people sort of find themselves already in the job sometimes?"

The trap was closing on him again. Whose side was she on? He felt betrayed. Desperate. "What are you trying to do to me?"

She gazed at him, infinitely sad. "You don't understand."

"No, I sure as hell don't!" Frank's shout was drowned in a great turmoil from the crowd around the doorway, a bustling of legionnaires at the open door.

"It's Magnus," Frieda yelled in Frank's ear. "They'll all be leaving now."

But Magnus, once inside, seemed in no hurry to go. He poured himself a bowl of mead and drained it in one long pull, then poured another. He patted Fat Mama's voluptuous tummy and strode around the vinyl floor on hobnailed shoes, blessing the men and laying hands on the women, while they all pulled on long boots, his thin voice piercing the general din.

As Magnus made his rounds, the noise level increased, the hunters' excitement getting wilder. He passed close by, glanced at Frank, looked away, glanced back, squinted at him. It was as if the two of them were all alone in the room, Magnus's suspicious eyes stabbing through his disguise.

"Yes," Magnus said softly. He walked away.

Frank felt the rustling fear again. It was a companion now, a condition of life. He hated it.

The hunters had their boots on and were ready to leave. They all had guns, and some carried eight-cell flashlights. It was broad daylight.

What did he mean, "Yes"?

At a sign from Magnus, everyone quieted. Fat Mama presented him with what looked like a skull and poured it full of something red and steaming. He raised it solemnly. "To success in the hunt! And to victory on Tuesday! For Scorpio, God, and Country! Skoal!"

The booted men and women stirred and shouted: "Skoal!"

Magnus drank it off and wiped the red drippings from his chin. He looked at Frank again.

He knows. He must know.

When Magnus left at last, the hunters cheered and began tramping out of the inn after him. Frank grabbed a napkin and mopped sweat off his face. "What . . ." he began; but Frieda anticipated the question.

"They're after the gold, of course. Most Sundays there's a gold rush. It's part of it."

"Here, in Indiana? Gold?"

"There are lots of rumors. Stories of the buried treasure. They go after it whenever the other hunts fail."

"What treasure?"

"Some say one thing, some say another." She shrugged, as if tired of the subject. "Anyway, they're sure it's down there, somewhere, in the caves." And she added, with finality, "But they won't find it."

She shrugged again, and her tawny bracelets clinked a little.

SIX

WHAT WAS IT with her, Frank wondered later, slinking along behind her toward the church. Sunday evening: afterward, she
had said. He obediently kept his distance, blanket under his arm, her
runaway father's shoes trudging uphill.

Inside the empty church he could finally risk speaking. "It's only
to be together, to be alone together. So what was wrong with the
motel, the nice clean beds?"

She glanced back at him in that ambiguous way she had, but didn't
answer. She led him down to the basement, then through the long
stone tunnels, her candle flickering ahead, down to the cool limestone maze. And he followed. Led around by the nose, he thought.
Not the first time—by every woman he'd ever stumbled into bed
with. And why had none of it ever really mattered, all those golden
afternoons, bright with silky hair and musky skin and silent promises
that left so little behind? What was wrong with all of them? What
was wrong with him? Why was Nancy's face so hard to remember?

I am to teach you how to love: that strange intensity, the secrets in
the shadows of her eyes, candles in the labyrinth, stony steps deep

into the menacing earth—and finally the flickering image of Frieda, kneeling by the giant stalagmite.

Claustrophobia squeezed at his chest.

Then her arms were cool on his neck. He shivered. She unbuttoned his shirt, and he took it off. She opened his trousers; he took them off, and then his shorts.

He undressed her slowly, buttons on the plaid shirt, zipper on the jeans, the panties sweetly damp. She stood patiently, waiting till he was finished, then touched his nakedness with her calloused fingertips, contemplating him abstractly, as if he were marble. Her pale body glimmered in the candlelight, almost translucent. He touched her hair, too feverish to dare touching her skin.

Moments hovered in the shadows.

They knelt on the blanket, and her cool skin tingled against his. He kissed her softly, the merest brushing of lips, then leaned down to kiss her breasts, a small caressing of the tongue as she caught her breath and pressed against him, all curves and roundnesses. Easing her down, he nuzzled his face into the pillows of her thighs and gently made love to her other lips, teasing her tumid sex with the rough and smooth of his tongue until her body arched and she moaned softly. "Come," she whispered, "come." He entered her. Their bodies made a quickening rhythm, then deep and breathless tremors, then a steady, valedictory motion as peaceful as tropical seas.

The rhythm continued as if outside them, universal, a pulsing that would never cease. A lifetime happened. Frieda's voice was a sigh. "My sweet Aquarius."

Frank felt himself wither; the rhythm stopped. His voice had the lilt of a *castrato*. "Must you always say that?"

"What?" She sounded startled.

"That superstition? Even here? Now?"

She stood up quickly. The bruised look: handle with infinite care, drop the subject, for God's sake, not the time or the place.

But he went on with it, perverse. "Don't you see, it's all such nonsense, that stuff about stars and planets, prehistoric nonsense at that."

The lovely body in candlelight was a study in anatomy, muscles stiffening with anger. "I didn't know you were an atheist."

He wasn't ready for that, hadn't made the connection, not consciously. "Atheist?"

"Scoff if you want to, like Olaf and his heretics, we're used to it." Her voice burned at him; she was not good at playing humility.

The whole scene was so grotesque, such an argument, in such a place, in such a position. He sat up, tried to bring her back to him. "I'm not scoffing. It's just a matter of common sense, of seeing things as they are."

"I see *you* as you are, and I'm sorry for you." She turned away from him and stood stiffly, her tight buttocks at eye level inflaming him again, confusing him.

"I mean seeing reality, not fantasies." He tried to keep his voice steady. "Listen, I'm sorry I brought it up right now, but it upsets me to think of you being taken in by all that hocus-pocus."

She took a barefoot step or two away from him, and he wanted to reach out, hug her naked knees, stop the bickering, not hurt her any more. He pitied her outrage, her warped indignation. When she turned around, her small breasts trembled in the candlelight.

"You talk that way not because you know any truth, not because you see any visions, but only in a pitiful certainty of objects, things, senses, the certainty of ants, the certainty of beetles."

"That's exactly backwards!" He wanted to stop himself, but couldn't. "There isn't any truth, any vision, when you just close your eyes and wish, when you put yourself in the hands of witch doctors."

She was going on as if he hadn't spoken. "And none of it matters unless you make a sign in the world, bring your godlike Aquarian dreams into the service of the One and the All. Faith, Frank, you have to have faith."

No, Frank wanted to shout, that's not it. Magic, humbug, come off it! He wanted to snap his fingers in her face, break the spell. He had reason on his side. Why wouldn't she listen?

"Right over there is a little pool." She pointed into the darkness. "The water is perfectly clear, and if you hold a candle over it, you can see cave fish, albino fish. They have eyes, the remains of eyes, but they've been blind for centuries. They move about down here with no trouble, because they've adapted. But still, they're blind."

Staring at darkness, he waited for the predictable moral.

"You're like that, too. You go through the world myopic and color-blind, doing all right, you think, but not realizing what you can't see."

Certainty, Frank thought, solemnity. What a blessing it is, not to be seventeen.

She seemed to have talked her anger away, and stood there in the candlelight seeming taller than before, fuller-bodied, one hand reaching out to him, maternal. A pause lengthened out to silence, and in the quiet of the cave, the guttering candle made a sound like beating wings. Somewhere in the gloom, a timeless dripping eased a new stalagmite into its long birth.

Nothing here was real—no gauges, no clocks, no calipers. The claustrophobia came back, crushing the breath out of him.

She took a step toward him. Another. She came down slowly to her knees, and her cold breasts nuzzled his cheeks. His eyes closed; his lips moved over her skin.

Why? Frank wondered. Why me? Then out loud, "So it matters to you that much?"

"Oh, yes, it matters, of course it matters. Your sincerity, your warmth, your kindness, your gentleness, above all your gentleness, it's all there in your Aquarian nature. Don't you see? Our feeling, our understanding, that—that divinity . . . Well, I just couldn't love anybody but an Aquarius."

Love? Frank felt a quick jab of panic.

"I wasn't going to tell you this, but now I warít you to know." She spoke slowly, awkwardly. "Last night, when we were together . . . Well, it was my first time."

So she had been crying.

Sadness fluttered through the cave on black wings. He stroked her cheek with the backs of his fingers.

Love?

But she didn't persist, and later it was all right again, the words abandoned, the rhythm resumed, the satiny rub of skin on skin, his tears on her cheeks, her eyes lighting the cavern blue.

Afterward, as the quiet minutes passed, Frank was still uneasy. Love? That throbbing of joy in the touch of a fingertip, that sharp twinge in the chest, the fear of death at the moment of consummation?

Nancy, Nancy, where are you tonight?

As he dozed off, he kept wondering, why are her hands so rough and hard?

SEVEN

E ARLY SUN outlined the expanse of Julian, hovering at Frank's
bedside.

"Up, boy, up," he barked. "This is no Caribbean cruise, we came
here to work."

Work? But it wasn't that easy, after last night. The blurry Julian
was tapping a thick file folder. Frank stalled. "How about you? Did
the sow's nipples do the trick?"

Julian huffed and puffed: "Sow's nipples, indeed. Psychological
flimflammery! Who needs it?"

"But I gather she was satisfied with your performance," Frank persisted, "since I notice you're holding what looks like parchment." He
hated to ask, but he had to. "Wong's?"

"They're always satisfied. Professional pride. Come along now, get
dressed and come over to my room. There's a lot to be done. Wong's,
yes, of course. Yes, indeed. Come on."

OK, it was morning. Frank went through the motions, showering
carefully, not wetting the beard, pulling on pants and shirt. He
yanked the curtains all the way open. Neon was blinking red.

The Steak and Lobster Inn
Motel   Cafe

Julian paced the room briskly, parchment in hand, all business. He jerked a thumb at the coffee maker, and Frank took the hint.

"Now listen, try to think dissertation for a while, think inflection, style. Listen to this. 'The voyaging had not been easy. The winds being perverse, we had to beat with our oars upriver, against the brutal current riding to the sea. The red-skinned skrälingar were sometimes fearful, sometimes bold, and more than once we had to put the war shields over the side and do battle with the countless skin-canoes. Always we were victorious in these skirmishes, but sometimes they cost us our best fighters, the flint arrows flying like murderous hail among us. Many a martyr was given to the muddy water on that voyage, or burned on an island pyre on dusky evenings, to the long wail of woeful warriors. Only the mysteries sustained our spirits in those bitter days, and the thought of Asgard and the central cave.' "

"Where did all that come from?" Frank had never heard it before.

"The new Viking parchments Sybil just gave me. But listen, there's more, get this. 'Then came the weary portages, bending our backs for the slaughtered oxen, the scalding summer beading our skin with salt, the red-skinned skrälingar's hatred harrying us in the tangled forests.

" 'At last the easy inland seas and safety, our dragon prows out of reach of the skin canoes, our sails filling with the welcome breeze, our path on the gentle waves pointing to the setting sun, until we found the north-running river. Then we held our prows against the current again, tired arms at the merciless oars, until we forked into the south-running river, and drifted safely to the land of the central cave.

" 'And there, the long hunt ended, our altars could be fired in noonday darkness, the holy bulls be burned again to God. The stars in their steady courses shed mercy on us all.' "

Stars. Frank groaned, thinking of Frieda's stubborn superstition. But he couldn't stop listening to Julian's voice, and he realized, reluctantly, that those ancient Vikings were finally getting under his skin.

" 'And the heavy burden of our rescue, the golden bowls and bucklers, the silver tankards and helmets, all the precious coins, and the jeweled medallions and brooches could find their final resting place in the tomb of the living God, where the consecrated lamp would never cease its burning.

" 'And over the central cave blazed the hunter by winter nights, the bear by summer. And at dawn on Midsummer Day the rays of the fiery lion fall directly through the twin stones and kindle the flames at the portals of the holy place, lighting the sacred way to the mystery, to the central cave, to the holy altar, to the treasures, a guide eternal to the faithful, that the central cave be never lost again.' "

A long pause made Frank look up. "You translated all that just now? This morning?"

"Golden bowls. Jeweled medallions." Julian seemed to drift off, then recovered. "But what a crazy mixup, did you ever hear anything like it? 'Mysteries'! 'Holy bulls'! 'Fiery lions'!" He snorted. "It's a cultural hash, an outrage."

"What's he after, Julian?"

"Huh?"

"Wong. What the hell does he want? What's his dodge?"

The question had hovered between them for eight hundred miles, irritating Frank, annoying Julian. Wong's covering notes were always perfunctory: enclosed-is-the-current-chapter-please-send-translation-immediately.

Julian was grave. "Look, why don't we just take his word for it? He needs my translations for a critical edition of these old parchments, another timeless and invaluable dissertation, right? Wong isn't the only failed scholar who happened to make a lucky find." Julian sighed and gazed at Frank. "What interests me more is that you always suspect fraud in other people. Why is that? Does it mean something about yourself?"

Frank bristled. "Listen, my father always said, wherever there's a buck, there's a bilk. And he was right. If you're not a shill, you're a gull, he always said." Was there a smell like garbage in the air? Frank squinted defiance at his disapproving uncle. Julian wasn't the only one who knew something about truth.

"I thought I saw signs of life in here." Fat Mama bumped the door open with her mighty backside and eased into the room, carrying a tray. She put it on a table and whipped off the linen cover like a magician. Behold: sweet rolls, bacon and eggs, toast, steaming coffee.

"Reward for services rendered." She winked at Julian. "You hear the one about the impotent Pisces and the nympho mermaid?"

"Yes, yes." Julian snickered obligingly.

"OK, well, we'll just get rid of this lukewarm piss," she boomed, emptying their coffee cups in the bathroom, "and pour you something civilized. Follow your instincts today, Taurus. Find out just how far you can go. Take risks if necessary. And remember, use caution at all times."

The smell of real coffee filled the room. Frank inhaled. A cup was placed in his hand. He sipped.

She'd make somebody a good mother.

Julian was torn between duty and desire. Desire, as usual, won a shutout. He put down the manuscript and eyed the sweet rolls with his customary all-purpose lust. "Sybil, you're an angel. A goddess."

She sat on the protesting bed and poured herself a cup. Frank loaded a plate with bacon and eggs. Julian, tearing at a Danish, asked with his mouth full: "Isn't there anything else you can tell me about Wong? How did he get that parchment to you?"

"I told you, I never heard of him till you asked. A kid brought the envelope. Never saw him before, either."

Julian squinted at her. "But you've lived here all your life. You must know every kid in town."

She shook her head. "Kids! Don't see the little bastards in church any more. All running after Olaf—sports cars, motorcycles, snowmobiles—no respect." She trailed off, staring at the floor, chewing slowly. Then she winked at Julian. "But the election's tomorrow. Then we'll see, won't we?" She stood up and walked over to Julian's chair. "I won't butt in any more, stud, I know you're working. Just didn't want you to starve before tonight."

She took his head in her hands and pressed it to her huge bosom. Julian breathed in ecstatically. Frank looked away, ashamed of his sudden lust.

"Bye-bye, Gemini. Work hard today. Trust your emotions." Her throaty laugh teased him as she shuffled out and closed the door behind her.

His uncle was sitting there glassy-eyed.

"Julian, let's get back to the city! To hell with this spaced-out little town. Think about our investment, all that high-priced hype, our double-page spread in the *Journal of Higher Ed.*! Think of the word of mouth we're losing, Julian. We're not out for a joy ride in the country, we've got responsibilities. All those doctoral candidates back in New York—Albany, Buffalo, Stony Brook—they need us, depend on us. Twenty big ones a month!"

Julian drifted back into his body. He looked at the food. "Remember what your daddy always said."

"I remember, that's what I'm saying. Let's get back where the action is, where there's a windfall in the morning mail. He always said, when you're not going ahead, you're going under. Slow horses are for dog food, he said."

Frank savored the old adages, felt good all over. He remembered his father bringing him the fatal glove, the Mickey Mantle Special. How could the practical man have guessed what dangers lurked in that supple leather pocket?

"That's not what I meant, son." Julian was sliding into the avuncular role that always made Frank itchy. "Listen, he spent his whole life trying to grab a clear million and hold on to it. And at the end, nobody would cash his checks."

"It wasn't his fault. Hard times, inflation, recession. You can't make stew out of stones, he used to say."

His father threw him a hard one: *whap.*

"Hard times, maybe. But partly it's always your own fault, too."

"What's all that got to do with us?"

"It has everything to do. Listen, have you ever had a check bounce? Worse, had one refused? It's the ultimate denial. Of yourself, of your own personal self." Julian was eating steadily now, regaining his composure, working his way through bacon and eggs. "There's nothing quite like it for wiping a person out. Your daddy, my poor little kid brother—he died at the end of his own hemp rope, yes. But do you know why?"

Julian inhaled deeply. Frank's heart was doing flips and cartwheels.

He burned one back at his father.

"He'd ceased to exist, that's all. *Nobody would cash his checks.*" Julian bit into toast and honey.

His father, always his father. Frank tried to call up the memory of his mother, withered like a flower in her youth, tried to remember her voice, her eyes, the feel of her arms. But he was only four when she died. Nothing survived.

Not even the glove. The Mickey Mantle Special, one day, had just disappeared.

"It's no use, son. Some things, some experiences, are death itself." Julian chewed thoughtfully for a moment. "Unless your sense of being goes deeper than hustle, deeper than the fast buck. Truth, Frank, truth is the only mistress who never plays you false."

He paused, still munching. "He was a fine man. In a way. A great man. In a way. He could sell anything, even in the recessions, with all that sincerity, the friendly twinkle in the eye, the dollar sign in the buttonhole. But your daddy . . ."

"Was never ashamed!" Frank blurted, rebelling. "My God, Julian, a man who never in his whole life apologized for anything! There are the weak and there are the strong, that's how he saw it."

"That's not what I was about to observe," Julian frowned.

"And the strong are rich *because* they're strong, and the weak— the weak get clawed, the way God intended."

His father: his father had stolen the glove. Must have.

"Listen, your daddy was a fine businessman. He struck fast and without warning, and when he'd made his killing and disappeared into the sunset, he was always carrying loot, like a Viking, but . . ."

"And damn it, he never looked back, never indulged himself in shame. There's no such thing as guilt-edged security, he always said. Well, isn't that what the dissertation scam is all about? A way of living in this world, of beating the crooks at their own game, of vindicating my father to the bleeding hearts, the old grand slam in the bottom of the ninth, the American way of life? Are you ashamed of it, after four years of sweat and profit?" He paused, panting. "So what the hell are we doing out here in this weird little tank town?"

"I was about to say that in the end, after the successes, the bond issues, the paper corporations, the wildcatting, the strip-mining— after all that, he ended up . . ."

"Broke, yes, I know that."

"Not just broke. Obliterated. He didn't really kill himself, you know, and your leaving didn't kill him either, not that one lousy season in the bush leagues."

"Don't try to con me, not about that!" The old scene rose in Frank's throat and choked him, that chunky body swinging from the terrace at dawn. "I turned my back on his life, refusing that partnership—made it all meaningless for him. I zapped him as sure as if I'd beaned him with a fast ball, he couldn't have tied that noose otherwise. There wasn't an ounce of remorse in his whole system." He noticed the quaver in his voice, and cleared his throat. "But I'll make it up to him."

"It doesn't matter, Frank, none of that. Remorse isn't the point. Shame, guilt, they aren't the point, because at the end it was all changed, all different. I promised him long ago, remember, that I'd take care of you, get you out of those cleats and into real business. I told him I'd make you a winner, and I have, haven't I? How many kids your age have their own six rooms on the fortieth floor? And a heated pool on the roof? And a Stingray in the ground-floor garage? Hmm? I mean, think about that for a minute, and trust me, because I'm telling you, long before the end, he was already gone, gone before you made your move to the minors, gone before he tied that rope to the balcony railing. Somebody was gone, *and your daddy didn't even know who was missing.*"

Frank didn't know what to say. Was that true? "I—I'll make it up to him. Somehow. Some things may take a lifetime to make up for, but I don't care, I won't stop till I make the big killing he always wanted to make . . ."

"It's an ugly memory. But look out here." Julian pulled back a curtain. In the distance the morning sun outlined a landscape of rolling hills and two incredibly steep crags that looked as if they had been carved with a knife. All the way from the murky eastern horizon to the silver Stingray just outside their window, the morning rush was on—Wildcats and Lynxes, Falcons and Eagles, Hornets and Sunbirds, Foxes and Road-Runners creeping along so slowly Frank could read the bumper stickers.

> I WILL GIVE UP MY GUN WHEN THEY PRY IT
> OUT OF MY COLD, DEAD FINGERS

Watching that scene was like looking at history. Frank got a lump in his throat. "Motors, my father used to say, V-8 engines, manliness—that's the past, present, and future of this country. We run on internal-combustion souls, always have, since the days of the one-cylinder chain-driven runabouts, the air-cooled V-4's, the flat-twin 'midships engines." Caught up in the feel of that long heritage, he let it all spill out. "Everything, all the way, the long, long way, from the retarded spark to electronic fuel injection, to syncromesh transmission, to power rack and pinion steering, dual carburetors, three hundred b.h.p. at six thousand r.p.m., shooting the quarter in fourteen seconds." He choked up, overcome by that magic vision, but cleared his throat and went on gamely. "Reclining bucket seats, Julian. Radial whitewalls. Chrome wire wheels, Mark IV air conditioning, hand-sewn top-grain leather upholstery, seven-litre twin-cam supercharged beauties cornering the switchbacks in Pennsylvania, Colorado, Oregon!" His voice was strong now, vibrant with the aspirations of an age, a continent. "So keep the faith, my father always said, stick to the two-fisted four-stroke performance, put your money on mineral rights, pipelines, petroleum. It's in our blood— it *is* our blood—grease is the song in our slippery hearts. The thousand-horsepower car slides through all our dreams as slick as heavy oil."

Julian broke in, his voice like a man with a gun. "Where are they all going, Frank?"

His mood shattered, Frank stared out the window, baffled. Slowly, with an effort, he recovered. "They know. We don't have to know, they know."

"Yes. That's what your daddy always said, you got it from him, didn't you? But pick a face, any face out there, and look right at it. Does it know? Does it understand? Does it seek any genuine truth, hear any clear melody, feel any real emotion?"

Frank sat down, sick. "And you say *I* suspect everyone of fraud."

"Well, that's why we're out here in this weird little town. All those monsters we've spawned—'The Effect of Conceptual Training on Reflective Tempo,' 'Stimulation of Temporary Threshold Shift,' 'Relative Stability of Regression Analysis'—they just finally got to me, that's all. Where the hell were they taking us?"

Frank tried to fight back, full count. "Right up there to the next bracket, that's where! My father always . . ."

"Listen, my little brother died in that noose with the questions still on his lips. 'Where?' 'What?' 'Why?' After all those years of big money, he not only had no cash or credit any more, he had no answers. Not even the simplest."

Frank scuttled off to the bathroom. The old fountains of guilt were flowing, pumping the bitterness into his throat.

"I'm sick of fantasies!" Julian shouted through the locked door. " 'Person Perception and the Locus of Social Variables'—I'm finished with all that. I'm going to find Wong and do this thing, do it right, every dreary footnote. *I'm going straight, Frank!*"

Frank gagged. His father's fault, all of it. Not his fault, his father's fault: the clean hemp line knotted to the terrace railing, the body dropping and dropping until the neatly tied noose . . .

Frank felt abandoned. Why could he never remember his mother's voice? He emerged from the bathroom and stood in front of the air conditioner. Ten deep breaths.

Julian was hunched over the dressing table, writing with one hand, still eating with the other. He stood up and poured Frank a cup of coffee. "Think about your professional life for a minute. No, think about your whole life for a minute, and you'll see what I've been talking about."

Frank knew what he meant, but he refused to be shamed. Julian's prose, after all, was hopelessly concise and clear. Frank, a Columbia Teachers College dropout, always had to give it professional respectability: to invert word orders, to garble contexts and referents, to invent parasociological terminology. Julian could manage this level of exposition for only a paragraph or two at a time, and then he would lapse into clarity, but Frank could sustain it for hundreds of pages, all consistently grave and obscure.

. . . investigate psycholinguistic-intensive dimensions of stepwise multiple regression analysis as a behavioral correlate of affective sensitivity in control subjects having significant amounts of comprehension variance in complex nonverbal life-test hypotheses . . .

They were a productive team, Julian and Frank, their talents neatly dovetailed.

Now, however, Julian seemed to have something more on his mind, something cunning. Frank recognized the symptoms, the sly glances, the solicitude.

"What, as you say, is Wong after? Will we ever manage to concoct a dissertation out of these runic riddles? Well, try this new Viking passage, just for style. 'Then came the weary portages, bending our backs for the slaughtered oxen, the scalding summer beading our skin with salt, the red-skinned skrälingar's hatred harrying us in the tangled forests.' How would you put that in dissertationese? How would you doctor that passage to please the jaded ears of an Ed.D. committee?"

Frank knew it was a trap, but he couldn't help himself, back in a rush at the office, Confidential Services, Inc., back at the old nine-to-five, Julian facing the wall, inventing statistics, Nancy at her desk by the window, voodooing the books for the I.R.S., and Frank in his usual creative daze, barely hearing the rumble of trains under Broadway, ignoring the half-eaten pastrami special floating on a sea of manuscript, and working from Julian's runic translations, the Viking poetry transmuted to solid prose, lead into gold. He improvised.

"The strategy of portaging was a mode of investigating the assumption that the role identity of oxen could be established as a dependent variable in the motivational model, the oxen having been subject to variances attributable to relative need in the preliminary studies. Heat, however, was *prima facie* an independent variable inversely related to group performance, and the identity concept of the indigenous inhabitants was a significant, though random, selectivity factor."

A truck backfired like artillery; he spilled coffee on the green carpet.

"You see what I mean, Frank?"

"What's the matter with it?" His voice sounded nasal to his own ears, somewhere between a shout and a whine. "It pulls an honest buck, doesn't it?"

"Honest? You call that honest?"

Frank dabbed at the brown stain in the carpet with a handful of motel Kleenex. "Uncle Julian, after four years, are you all of a sudden getting literary?" He made the word sound as indecent as possible.

Julian wasn't listening. "OLIIN," he said. "Something obviously wrong there."

"What's that?" Frank would never get used to Julian's abrupt changes of tack.

"Something queer about the whole thing. Look here."

Frank sighed and peered over the beefy shoulder. On a pad of motel stationery he saw the inscription.

"From the locket?"

Julian nodded.

"How did you get it?"

"Memorized it."

"God."

"Runes. Wong apparently has no monopoly on them out here in the sticks." Julian brooded. "Vikings in Indiana, think of it! Raiders, plunderers, the glut of Lindisfarne, all those monks with slit throats, red gushings in the cobblestone gutters, bags of silver, jeweled crucifixes."

"Julian, stick to the subject, will you?"

"The central cave, hmm. Look at this. When you transliterate the runes into Roman letters, you get OLIINVICT. What does that mean to you?"

Frank heard the baying of bloodhounds. He touched his beard nervously. The fear he had slept off with Frieda burned behind his eyes like a fever again.

"Nothing? OK, means nothing to me, either. But now remember the locket. Old-looking, wasn't it? Ancient, even. A gold too pure to wear well, no jewelry designer would use it now. But back then—twenty-four carats, soft as butter." Julian's voice had gone syrupy with desire. "Remember the edges of the locket itself—rounded, worn smooth. And the edges of the inscription?"

He was right, of course. Always right. It probably had been worn off at the edges.

"So think it through. What have we got there in the middle? OLIINVICT. Two I's together? Improbable. Impossible. Two words, then, at least. OLI INVICT. More like it. Now, let's work on the edges."

Julian's big paw swept up the last of the Danish. He munched for a moment.

"Start at the beginning. Boli? Doli? Foli? Loli? Noli—a possibility. Poli? Roli? Soli? Hmm, soli? Toli, voli . . . No, *soli*. It's a start, Frank. Soli, the sun. The sun!" He was getting agitated. "Freyr, god of the sun? Wait a minute. Look at the runes again." He studied the sheet of paper.

$$\text{ᛟᚱᛁᛁᚷᚠᛁᚲᛏ}$$

"The beginning of the second word has to be right—middle of the inscription, it's safe. But how did that word end? SOLI INVICT . . ." Julian burped resonantly. "*Soli invicto?* The unconquered sun?" Julian was up, now, pacing the little room. "Impossible. I mean, the whole context is wrong. Incredible."

As usual in the presence of Julian's leapfrogging intellect, Frank felt stupid. "I have no idea what you're talking about. Would you mind explaining . . ."

"How can I explain it when I can't believe it? Viking runes spelling out Persian mysticism? What is this, a hoax? I mean, it's incredible, that's all." Julian took a deep breath and looked at Frank soberly, as if he were making a great decision. "All right, to begin with—just to begin with—look out there again, out there in the street. Who are all those Hoosiers, anyway? Do you see any Orientals in that mob, anyone who might possibly be J. Randolph Wong? Or any Blacks, for that matter? Any swarthy Levantines? Puerto Ricans? Look close."

The rush-hour crowd moved past the window: pale-skinned people, many of them blond, some red-haired.

"Could you believe they're the direct descendants of Vikings?"

Frank laughed. Then looked again. Something in his chest froze solid.

"Could you believe they've been right here, right in this spot, since the year 1000 or thereabouts, keeping to themselves, minding their own business, turning away strangers? Right here in Ash Garden, Indiana?"

Frank grinned. The cold settled in.

"Ash Garden, my ass. Stop smirking and face it. You're in Asgard, son. Or as close to it as a mortal will ever get."

Frank sat down abruptly. Julian was registering a confusion of feelings—triumph, bewilderment, indignation.

"The trouble is, that's not the end of it. The trouble is, it's all botched. Somebody's been playing around with a lot of Eastern stuff, the garbage of mystery cults, and they've managed to screw it up beyond all recognition. The unconquered sun!" He snorted, paced, scratched his bald spot. "And whoever's sending us all this crazy stuff—well, I've got a feeling they're closing in on us."

He stopped. Frank sat motionless as absolute zero, not one molecule stirring. Somehow it hadn't occurred to him before: Julian was scared, too, as scared as he was.

Julian grabbed his arm, grinning a little too cheerfully. "Come on. First of all, let's go get us a real breakfast."

EIGHT

THE RESTAURANT was closed and locked, but at Julian's banging, Fat Mama opened the door. "Too goddam late for breakfast," spoke the beamy mistress of the Steak and Lobster Inn, "too goddam early for lunch. Try to be more prompt, schedule your time and activities wisely, don't be a slave to routine."

"Sybil, let's not be difficult." When it came to eating, Julian was no clock-watcher.

"Frieda! Special guests. Get the gentlemen's orders."

Frieda glided in from the kitchen with that charming awkwardness Frank remembered from his first sight of her, two days and many years ago. Her fingers caressed a table as she passed; then she leaned over and touched her cheek to Frank's, just above the false beard. The ice jam broke. He felt the blood jiggling in his veins. Fat Mama's insistent laughter dinged at his head.

He reached up and caught the small hand. "Sit with us."

She eased away, half bowing. "Oh, Mr. Freyr, you are the lord of the hostel here, and I am but your handmaiden."

Behind the grave mockery there was a supple, reedlike quality to her voice: Isfahan, houris, caravanserais in the desert. Frank stared. Vikings? Did Julian really expect him to believe these people were the offspring of Vikings? He reached for Frieda's hand again, but she moved away, holding a pad and pencil.

"Your orders, gentlemen."

Fat Mama's laugh rippled across the room. "The link sausages, Julian. Specialty of the house. Surefire, like the sow's nipples."

Frank made a mental note: avoid the sausage.

Julian ordered coffee, grapefruit, buckwheat cakes, eggs over light, fried potatoes, cornmeal muffins, and a double order of link sausages. Frank asked for orange juice.

Julian's train of thought had not been broken. "Vikings picking up the Latin is easy enough to figure. Could have happened anywhere, any time, all over Europe. Inevitable, in fact. Transliterating it all into runes naturally follows. Half the runes were cribbed from Latin in the first place, that's no problem. No, the problem's this other thing, the foreign stuff, the Oriental mysticism. I mean, there isn't any culture route, from Persia to Scandinavia. The unconquered sun, good God." He sipped his coffee, brooding.

Frank gazed at Frieda and listened, curious in spite of himself, as Julian rambled on.

"How the hell could it have happened, the mysterious East shunted all the way up there to Sweden? Through the Romans, maybe? But Varus's legions were cut to pieces way back in A.D. 9, and those bird-picked bones set the limits of empire in the North forever—trade routes wiped out." He scowled. "And how about the other end of it? Vikings once reached Byzantium, then cruised the coasts of Vinland, sure, but that was a thousand years later, too late to explain anything. No wonder Wong needs help. *I* need help."

"Julian, would you mind not talking about Wong? While we're eating?"

"You're not eating, I'm eating." Julian inhaled. "Did you ever hear of Mithra, the Persian sun-god, underground lord of the Roman legions?" He snorted, not waiting for an answer: "The unconquered sun, indeed."

Frieda had been drifting in and out of the kitchen with platters of food, grapefruit, orange juice, coffee and muffins, potatoes and bacon, buckwheat cakes and eggs, and finally the sausage.

Julian ate with a steady intensity that marked a fevered mind. "I mean, where could they have made the contact, the exchange? At the Roman frontier, maybe? The empire stretched from the mouth of the Rhine to the mouth of the Danube. And in the gap between those rivers were the Limits, the *Limes*, three hundred miles of ditches, palisades, forts, the Maginot Line of Rome, manned by all those pious legionaries, carrying their superstitions with them. It's a possibility."

The small calloused hand slid into his, her lips touched the back of his neck. Frieda sat down demurely and opened his hand, traced the telltale creases.

"Oh, Frank, what a palm you have! Look at this girdle of Venus, the lines of affection."

Frank closed his hand over her dirty fingernails. "I don't want to hear it." And his voice added, "I love you, Frieda."

She looked at him strangely. He was startled. He wasn't used to having his voice make decisions for him, springing them on him like this. In all his life he'd never said those words before. Had he, unexpectedly, without even knowing it, freed himself from Jessie Bell at last? Was it, this time, going to be different?

I am to teach you how to love.

Julian was eating and muttering, unaware of their presence.

"I love you, too. My sweet Aquarius."

His throat went tight. He tried to say it gently. "Frieda, can't you just leave it between us, and not keep dragging in the stars and planets?"

Her outrage flared up, and he felt the pain of it in his own chest.

"But it's your soul. You can't just shrug it off."

"Why don't we let my soul take care of itself?"

"It's already done. It was defined the day you were born, tolerant, kind, thoughtful, gentle, sensitive. All the things an Aquarius is."

"Frieda . . ."

"And we're perfect for each other, air and water, my domesticity to your humanitarianism, your friendliness to my possessiveness, my practicality to your generosity . . ."

"Frieda, cut it out, for God's sake!"

The shock in her eyes, like someone slapped. She looked down, struggling against her anger.

When she looked up again, she was smiling. "My patience to your vile temper."

He laughed, and their hands met again. Clocks stopped ticking all over Indiana.

Julian was working his way through stacks of buckwheat cakes, saving the potent sausages for dessert. "Who knows, it may have been some lost Gothic culture artery, running north like an overland Gulf Stream, carrying the Mithraic flotsam up from Persia, through Phrygia, Thrace, Sarmatia." He thought about it, swallowed, and shook his head. "But I doubt it. No, if there was a connection at all, if this whole thing isn't some demented Hoosier's idea of a practical joke, then they probably made the contact somewhere along the *Limes*, where all those superstitious legions were bleeding sacrificial bulls in their underground caves, marble Mithreums, waiting for the death of empire in their decadent jeweled barbarian helmets, Rome in the death-hug of the Orient."

Bulls. Death. Something furry crept along Frank's spine.

Julian chewed thoughtfully, savoring eggs and speculation. "Or maybe—maybe later, after the fall, at that fracture in history when the Oriental cults stayed on in Europe, in the wake of the fugitive legions, and the Viking raids were just beginning—a seductive mysticism, picked up by those fierce heathen and cherished, then held in the culture, in the blood, in the racial memory, for centuries, purged from the homeland at last by Christian zealots wiping the North clean of paganism, but preserved in those long ships cruising the St. Lawrence." His voice had gone slow, wistful.

Julian suddenly attacked the sausages, as if emerging from a dream. "Preposterous. Absurd!"

Outside, the baying hounds were getting louder. Frank felt his beard. Frieda smiled at him, and in the nimbus of that smile he feared death more than ever. She whispered: "If you're an Aquarius, you must be an activist, right?" The question was so unexpected that he could only stare at her. "Have you done any anti-draft counseling? Picketed any nukes? Have you been in any abortion-rights marches? E.R.A. rallies?"

He laughed, but nervously. "Not my style, I guess."

She wouldn't be put off. "I forgot, you're older. How about demonstrating against the war? Did you ever occupy any college buildings? March on the Pentagon? Speak at teach-ins?"

Fat Mama interrupted, bringing hot coffee, and Frank silently blessed her. She pinched Julian's cheek and patted Frank's beard. Squinting at it critically, like an artist, she admonished Frieda. "You should brush it again, baby. Keep it looking natural, just in case. Matter of life and death, maybe. If those bastards make a move, it'll be before the election, before tomorrow."

Activism? Demonstrations? A matter of life and death? He was in deep, way over his head. Frank listened to the bloodhounds, and the fear grew in him till he could smell it, like something left too long in the oven.

Frieda had left the room, and Fat Mama was talking to Julian. "If you're so crazy about the locket, love, take a look at Frieda's bracelets when she comes back. Hey, you ever hear the one about the Portuguese Scorpio and the Spanish fly?"

"Yes," Julian leered, "yes, yes, a good one, very funny. What about the bracelets?"

Frank sipped his orange juice. Fresh, of course, and delicious. Fat Mama made him homesick for a home he'd never had but always imagined, where the kitchen was warm on winter days with the smells of baking pies, where fresh fruit sat around in big glass bowls and didn't spoil, where the faithful coffeepot made everybody brothers and sisters, in the care of an aproned angel whose voice you would always, always remember.

Frieda was back, bending over him. She worked his whole beard with a soft brush, combed his hair, and then held his chin in her left hand like a head dissociated from its body, patting and shaping it with her right hand. Frank loved it.

"There, now. Your own mother wouldn't recognize you, you're so distinguished."

"Thanks a lot."

"Don't be a smart-ass, Frieda," Fat Mama chided. "Come show Julian your pretty bracelets."

She rounded the table, a little off balance, like a slightly tipsy dancer. When Julian saw the gold bracelets up close, he stared. Trembling, he reached out and turned the widest bracelet. Then he pulled out his notebook and scribbled in it, copying the runes.

ᚠᛒᛉᚱᛁᛌ�ᛏᛌᚠᛈᛟᛉᛁᛟᛌᛉᛏᚪᛈᛉᛒᛟ

When he looked up, he was as suspicious as a night watchman: "Your mother gave them to you, Sybil?"

Fat Mama said nothing.

"You have nothing else to tell me? Your mother?"

She bridled. "If you're going to hassle me, I won't say another word. I told you, my mother, yes. Her mother before her. What's so goddam freaky about that?"

Through his obvious irritation, Julian actually seemed embarrassed, a rare event. "I didn't mean to be offensive. It's just incredible, that's all."

Fat Mama got up in an elaborate huff, stalking around the table. She reminded Frank of the stately Sybil at Magnus's sacrifice. A cold wind blew across his face.

"No, I'm sorry. I didn't mean incredible, I meant unusual. It's extraordinary, is what I meant."

Frieda flourished on anger, but Fat Mama held no grudges. She laughed till the skin rippled on her doughy arms. "Shit, Taurus, you do babble a lot. You should listen more, talk less, concentrate on the job at hand. Come on, tell me what you wrote there. What does the incredible bracelet say?"

Frieda came back to Frank's side and sat down, leaning her head against his shoulder.

Julian studied his paper briefly. "*Ab oriente ad occidentum*," he quoted, drily. "From the East to the West."

He looked from Frieda to Fat Mama, squinting a little, like a man who thinks he's being had. Fat Mama sipped her coffee, impassive. Frieda looked at Frank with grave blue eyes that had just taken on the shape of almonds.

NINE

THE BAYING DOGS sounded very close, and suddenly there was a burst of gunfire. Fat Mama got up and looked out the window. "What's going on? They're shooting off their damn guns, down there at the corner of Elm Street."

She checked to make sure the front door was locked, then quickly closed the Venetian blinds. Burst after burst of gunfire rattled through the street. The dogs sounded frantic.

Fat Mama was pacing about. "God damn it, what's all the shooting about? Just who the hell do they think they are?"

"Men," Frieda muttered, "men!"

Frank felt the guilt settling on him like soot.

Soon there was a furious hammering at the door. Fat Mama was indignant, insult to injury. "Get away!" she shrilled. "We're not open!"

But the banging continued. Someone was yelling, his words drowned out by gunfire. At a pause in the shooting, the voice came through clearly. "Open up, Sybil! It's me, Olaf."

Olaf? Sheriff Olaf?

The others want you dead.

Strange nerves and muscles began working under Frank's skin, some primitive circuitry, the twitching of hide on a horse's flank. "I'd better get out of here."

But Fat Mama had already opened the door, and Olaf stumped in, half dragging, half carrying a young man in khaki. He eased the limp figure onto the floor. "Johanssen got it in the legs. Passed out. See what you can do, Sybil. And call the ambulance. He's too good a man to lose."

Frieda was on the phone. Fat Mama got the man's pants off. Blood oozed across the vinyl tile. "God, it's more like shrapnel than bullets." She tore strips off a tablecloth for tourniquets, and bound the injured legs. "He's in shock. It's a bad day for Leos. Leos shouldn't even get out of bed on a day like this." She covered him with tablecloths, tucked him in.

"He's a Libra," Olaf objected, slumping into a chair.

"Oh. Well, it's a bad day for Libras, too. What the hell's going on out there, anyhow?"

Olaf sounded angry but tired, the profound weariness of an old man. "Some of Magnus's Legion perverts. I've never seen it like this before. This whole campaign's getting out of hand."

He wiped his face with a red handkerchief.

"We worked them over, though. Don't think any of them got away. Damn it, we're going to have law and order around here if I have to exterminate every legionnaire in Ashland County. Shrapnel, for God's sake!"

Frank was trying to keep calm, but his coffee cup rattled. Olaf squinted at him. "You're new around here, aren't you, fella?"

Fat Mama looked up. "These two gentlemen are guests of mine, Olaf, here for the fair. Boys, this is our sheriff, Big Olaf."

Frieda was back, sitting beside Frank, humming an indistinct tune.

"You look familiar," Olaf said. The old eyes were piercing, but Frank knew by the squint they were myopic. It was reassuring somehow, vain old man without glasses. "Can't place you, though." He settled in his chair, looking back and forth from Frank to Julian. "Where you from?" He smiled, showing an expanse of sturdy false teeth, making the question casual and friendly, like a lingerie sales-man at a convention.

"New York," Frank and Julian said, almost together.

Fat Mama handed Olaf a cup of coffee, then checked the wounded man.

"Really? And how'd you happen to hear about our little county fair, way back east?"

Frank felt spotlights burning in his face. Julian spoke up, a little too fast. "Just driving by, sheriff. Vacation, you know, no hurry. Saw the road signs and decided to stop. For amusement."

"I see." Olaf sipped his coffee. "Not here on business, then?"

"No, no, not at all."

"Business takes a license in this county, you know. From my office."

"No business, sheriff."

Olaf was squinting at him again with those severe precinct-house eyes. Sweat eased down Frank's armpits. Then Olaf got up. "Well, that's fine. Amusement, hmm? Hope you find it. I hope you find all the amusement you can use." He paced for a moment, then squinted at Frank again. Frank felt himself blushing under the false hair.

"No, the fellow I'm thinking of was younger. Didn't have a beard, either." Olaf walked toward the door, but seemed reluctant to leave. He kept squinting from Frank to Big Mama and back again.

Frank tightened his stomach muscles, an isometric exercise: hold on, hold together till he gets out the door. His right heel was making a rapid drumbeat on the floor. With a prodigious effort of will, he stopped it.

A siren was getting closer, louder. "Here's the meat wagon now." Olaf opened the door and stood there a moment, looking at Frank. "I'll be seeing you," he said softly.

Frank could tell he meant it.

TEN

"AN OLD MOVIE," Julian grumbled after the stretcher bearers were gone. "We've stepped right into a B-movie thriller. Worse than that, even. Into the third verse of some god-awful country music." He paced around, irritated. "And that man knows a lot more about us than he's admitting. What the hell is this cat-and-mouse game all about?"

Frank relaxed his desperate control and slumped in his chair, head in hands.

Julian socked a fist in his palm. "What gets me isn't the sheriff so much. You might expect some deputy to come sniffing around, checking your hotel registration, your out-of-state plates, all that. It's how J. Randolph Wong knows we're here that I can't figure out." Julian's irritation turned itself on Fat Mama. "The 'treasures,' the 'mysteries'! *Ab oriente ad occidentum!* It really *is* incredible."

"There you go again."

"Sorry, Sybil. But damn it, where's Wong getting this stuff, anyway—crackling old parchment, faded runes? There must be a hoard of it around here somewhere. And you, with all your 'pretty bracelets,' I'll bet you know where it is."

Fat Mama wiped busily at a table.

Julian pulled from his pocket the translation of Wong's latest installment. " 'At dawn on Midsummer Day the rays of the fiery lion fall directly through the twin stones and kindle the flames at the portals of the holy place.' "

He looked at Frieda and at Fat Mama, studying each of them like a man who has been plotted against. "Twin stones? What twin stones? The two spires of that church on the hill? How old is that place anyway?" He paused; no one said anything. "What we have to do," he finally declared, "is go back to that cave under the church. The place where you hid Frank."

Fat Mama's voice was as level and toneless as a threat. "You're taking it all too literal-minded. And you're acting like this Wong character was the official historian of Ash Garden, and you don't even know if he lives here. Caves? There are caves all over southern Indiana."

She brightened. "Listen, you're on the brink of a new cycle today. Good lunar aspect, sense of perceptiveness heightened, Mars transiting Jupiter. You're on the verge of great discoveries. So do yourself a favor. Stay the hell out of the church."

Julian shrugged it off. "Wong is keeping track of us somehow, wherever he is, and he needs us for something, God knows what. He needs my translations pretty badly, or he wouldn't go to all this trouble. One way or another, he's bound to show up, wanting his parchment back, and by then I've got to have some things figured out. There may not be much time left. Let's go."

"It's only a story. You're doing all this for a bundle of make-believe." Fat Mama's eyes were shadowed, as though she had pulled the blinds inside them.

But Julian was determined. He took her arm and began to lead her to the door. "Come on, let's get started."

She blew up. "You Taurus bastards are impossible! I'm trying to reason with you, and all you can give me is this diehard mulish cussedness. You're nothing but a bullheaded Taurus prick!"

"Hold it," Julian laughed. "I'm not a Taurus."

"What's that?"

"Frank was just teasing you when we registered at the motel. I'm a Capricorn."

Frieda looked at Frank, startled. Fat Mama choked as if someone were strangling her. Then her eyes narrowed, gleaming in triumph. "Son of a bitch!" she crowed, "I knew there was something fishy about you. All that organization, that practicality, that compulsive talkativeness. Why, of course you're a Capricorn!" Her boisterous laughter played over the little group like a waterfall. "I see it all now—Capricorn ascending, the moon in Virgo, Saturn in the ninth house, Mars retrograde, Uranus sextile the ascendant. I can read you like a book—ambitious, energetic, calculating, intellectual, charming, aloof. Oh, don't tell me you're not a Capricorn." She laughed and laughed. "Well, for a Capricorn you're not such a bad guy. But this stuff about caves and twin stones and fiery lions, it's all just a story. I tell you again, for your own good, forget it."

Julian got up and went to her, put his arm around her from behind, and squeezed her to him, their massive forms fusing like sponges. "A 'story'? I'll tell you a story, a story of Vikings—fierce big-breasted blondes and men with broadswords, axes, and fire, a story that began a thousand years ago, in the great temple at Uppsala, where Freyr, god of the sun and god of fertility, stood nude and noble in the north wind, displaying to all worshipers his mighty phallus, symbol of the peace and pleasure he breathed down upon mortals."

They were rocking gently to the rhythm of his voice. He eased her toward the door, her resistance melting.

"A story that started in the mists of the northern oceans, Vikings on the uncharted iceberg sea, driven by storms so fierce that many brave voyagers were lost forever, but bringing at last, to the barbarous shores of the unknown world, the sacred Nerthus, mother earth herself, and bringing also giants, monsters, demons of the frost and of the wind off the cold fens."

Julian went on talking while Fat Mama, with the air of a conspirator (but conspiring with them, Frank wondered, or against them?), left the restaurant and led them through the streets, past the chain stores and used car lots, uphill to the twin-spired church, then through the secret doors again, and down, down.

"Victorious in every battle with the red-skinned skrälingar, after the invocation of the holy warlike names, the shrieking poetry of the skalds, men and women going into battle together, needing no shield, no mail, so fierce, berserk with the rage of wolves, that neither fire nor spears dismayed them."

Julian talked all the way down the stairs and down the long tunnels, stalactites ghostly around them, the rush and flutter of bats, the music of lost rivers, to the forbidden steel door, Fat Mama, with a key, squeezing through first, then Julian and Frieda and Frank, who stared at the unbelievable sight: the long ship chocked on its ancient keel, perfect in every plank, from the fierce golden dragon at the bow to the long steering board at the stern, the red sail faded but intact, oars in place, symmetrical. And chained at the helm, the tall skeleton, peering out of hollow eyes and pointing ahead, ahead, ahead, with his fingers of naked bone.

ELEVEN

FRIEDA shuddered, staring at the bony figure in candlelight.
"Lucky!"

"Loki?" Words caromed and echoed through the cave as Julian strode around the hull, inspecting it. "Loki was fettered in his cavern, yes. But this fine fellow is punished by no poisonous serpent."

His talk was only to cover the silence, Frank realized, to occupy them while he occupied himself.

"The Viking burial caves," Julian called from the far side of the ship, "were always rich with treasures, a shipload of precious cargo for Valhalla, gold, ivory, silver bowls, coins, medals, jeweled swords."

Fat Mama stood alone, impassive. But then, Frank reasoned, she had seen it all before.

"What does it mean, Sybil?" Julian finally asked, finished with his poking about the long ship. When Fat Mama remained silent, he went on. "That's a real Viking ship, all right, but this whole thing's too stagey. Who set it up?"

"You asked me to bring you here, and I did, Capricorn."

Julian was intrigued and piqued, a mood Frank recognized, the scholar frustrated. "Where's the gold, the loot? And why isn't this poor guy flat on his back, as he should be? Where's his wreath of garnets? Who put him up to this Longfellow pose?"

Questions, questions, Frank thought. Will we ever get any answers?

Fat Mama said nothing. Julian spoke to Frieda with a calculated gentleness. "Remember the story you told Frank yesterday? About the trolls, and Armin, the scorpions, the friar, all in the central cave? Well, go on, what else do you know about it?"

Frieda thought a moment before she answered. "It was just a story, a folk tale, to teach us about ourselves, not really about caves or bulls."

"Nonsense!" Julian's impatience shattered his fragile courtesy. "There's more to it than that. This is hill country, cavern country. Don't you know what that means?"

"She knows nothing yet, she's only guessing. This is her first visit to the altar."

"Altar?" Julian pounced on the word. "Altar? That flat stone at the prow?"

Fat Mama shrugged.

"And what, may I ask, is sacrificed there? Well, Sybil? Well, Frieda?"

"She knows nothing, I tell you. Only the men come here. And certain women. This is her first time. I let her come today because tomorrow, Midsummer Day, is her eighteenth birthday, and she'll be obliged to come."

"Obliged?"

"The women of my family. My mother. Her mother before her. Now Frieda."

Fat Mama looked away. Frieda spoke, a rush of words. "Lucky killed the bull at the last election, four years ago. Somebody always does it, one way or another. And that's why he's here. He was chosen, at the fair. The lucky one is always king for a day, until . . ." She hugged Frank hard, but wouldn't look at him.

"You'll get them all mixed up, Frieda, let me tell it." Fat Mama stood by the prow of the ship, tall and somber. Her voice took on a stately cadence Frank hadn't heard before. "In the days when Loki walked this earth, he risked, in the guise of a mortal, many strange and perilous adventures. One Midsummer Day he rode out of the mountains and beheld a beautiful but troubled city. As he entered its gates, a huge black bull charged at him, which, had he been human, would surely have cost him his life. Loki, however, with his giant's strength, soon stabbed the bull to the heart.

"Then all the lords and ladies of the town came forth with lutes and singing, to strew flowers in his path.

" 'Why do you greet me so courteously?' asked the giant. 'Why,' came the response, 'because you have saved us from the scourge of the bull and are therefore become our king and our god.'

" 'That is passing pleasant,' replied Loki. 'And who, pray, is to be my queen?'

" 'You are to choose, yourself, from the fairest of our maidens,' spoke the townspeople, 'and you will enjoy her for twenty-four hours, after which you are to be chained in the holy cave forever, in the manner of our tradition.'

" 'Nay,' shouted the giant, 'need have I none of such a kingdom! Need have I none of such an honor.' "

Her rich voice faltered to silence.

"Well?" Julian prompted. "Did they succeed in 'honoring' him or not?"

Fat Mama hesitated. "Some say one thing, some say another. Some say it wasn't Loki at all, but Freyr."

"Freyr? *Freyr*? But that's the whole point, damn it!" Julian was furious. "Look, the king was slain at Uppsala at every festival, the dying god and all that, yes, yes. But are you telling me that's why Frank has to go around sporting that woolly beard? I mean, you can't lead up to something like that, and then just drop it."

But Fat Mama was silent, her great arms folded, eyes half closed like a Bodhisattva.

Julian seemed not so much angry now as exasperated, determined. "All right, then, by God, I'll do it myself, somehow. All you cryptic Hoosiers, Wong, and the rest of you, I didn't come all the way out here just to end up a patsy translator of old parchments. It's understanding I'm after. I'm going to get the truth in spite of your myths and your 'mysteries.' "

He rounded the long ship once more, then headed for the door, walking now with a slight list, like an old man. His voice was pitifully scratchy. "Come on, let's get back to daylight."

Fat Mama held out a hand to Frieda, who was shivering a little. She shook her head. Fat Mama looked at Frank for a moment as if she were reading his mind. "Take practical steps toward your goal, but keep your emotions in check today. Frieda, pull the door shut tight, afterward."

When the sound of their footsteps faded, Frank set Frieda's candle on the smooth limestone and led her toward the bony ghost, led her, trembling, closer and closer, and finally eased her onto the smooth, cool rock, and there, under that petrified grin, kept his emotions in check and gently loved her till all her shudders stopped.

TWELVE

FRIEDA yawned and stretched, arms over head. Her small breasts lifted, and Frank felt the miracle again, the tingling. He reached for her, but she leaned away and picked up her clothes. Fumbling in the pockets, she found a watch.

"Damn, we're late."

Frank was startled. "Late for what?"

"The tea party."

The runaround again. He gritted his teeth, determined to ask no more questions. They dressed without talking, the soft rustle of clothes echoing the circling bats. He was cold.

Halfway up the long ascent, he couldn't stand it any longer. "All right, Frieda, where are we going? What's this 'party' routine?"

She turned back to him, the candle casting shadows above her cheekbones. "I thought you'd never ask."

"Well, are you going to tell me?"

"Partly tell, partly show." She sounded impatient. "We're going over to the park, to throw some tea in the ocean."

"Thanks, that helps a lot."

She turned and resumed the long climb, walking briskly. "You know anything about diesels?"

He shrugged. "A little."

"Then you're one of us." It was a dare. The anger was on her again.

The tunnels finally ended, and they crept through the deserted church and furtively out into the street. Night traffic moved by. Frieda kept slightly ahead, avoiding lights, taking side streets and alleys, talking in a low, intense voice.

"I was serious when I asked you about the demonstrations, Frank. It's important to me. I'd just like to know—as a good Aquarius, I suppose you're always fighting for the rights of underdogs, for blacks, latinos, women?"

Guilt mushroomed in his throat, dank as a cellar: "Not—lately."

"Whales, then? The snail darter?" He shook his head. "Oh. Well, I'll bet you send checks to Planned Parenthood, don't you? The Sierra Club? The ACLU? The NAACP? NOW? And you gave up lettuce during the strike? And stopped eating tuna to save the dolphins? And wrote to the papers about toxic wastes?"

He trudged along, head down. The mildew was spreading green across his unworthy soul. His silence was a confession.

She seemed to take pity on him. Stopping in a dark side street, she cupped his face in her hands and brushed the damp hair off his forehead. He put down the picnic basket and pulled her against him, her warmth on his chest a terrible burden of love. She nibbled his earlobe and whispered, "What is it, then? You just don't like to get involved, is that it? You don't like playing God? Well, anyway you must have your private opinions. How do you feel about sexual harrassment? White-collar crime? Overpopulation? The military-industrial complex?"

He was throbbing with confusion, aroused by her touch, baffled by her bizarre catechism. He broke away and picked up the wicker basket.

She was already striding along, but she wouldn't stop talking. "If you're not part of the solution, you must be part of the problem, right? If *you* aren't out there saving the world, who is? If *you* aren't playing God, who else is?"

He kept his head down. Some questions have no answers.

They were in a dark alley. She stopped beside a little one-car garage and rapped impatiently, four times, on the lid of a garbage can. Then twice more. Immediately the door opened and two figures emerged.

"You're late."

"Who's this?" Both of them stared at Frank. The mushrooms of guilt burgeoned under their suspicious gaze.

Frieda's voice crackled like a C.B. "Frank. He's OK, a friend. Frank, this is Kent, Sigrid." She jabbed with her thumb.

Kent was a tall boy with a sparse mustache, probably still in high school. Sigrid looked a little older, and taller than any of them, her hair a long blond braid. Like Frieda, she seemed irritable; a permanent frown creased the middle of her forehead. "How do you know he's OK?"

Frieda stared her down, her voice still tinny and sharp. "Trust me, all right? He's an Aquarius. We'll get started, then you'll see. Get the gear."

Kent took the picnic basket, went back inside the garage, and came out with long-handled wrenches, pocket flashlights, wire cutters, and what looked like a sandbag. Everybody carried something. Frank hoisted the bag. "What's this?"

"Sugar."

"Fifty pounds of it? What kind of tea party you throwing?"

Kent laughed, an easy, relaxed sound. "Very useful stuff."

Frieda gestured briskly. "OK, move out. We'll follow."

They slunk down the alley, five paces apart, Frank and Frieda behind them, side by side. "We've got cadres all over town, small groups like this one. But we only move sporadically, so they never know when or where we'll hit."

"Who's 'we'?"

"Environmental Resistance Groups. We hate all this." She gestured angrily at nothing. At the air. "We fight it the only way we can, the only way that's left to us. The law's always on their side, the best law money can buy. Listen, maybe you weren't much of an activist before, but we're going to give you a chance to be one tonight." She hesitated. "That is, if you want to."

"Well, sure." He swallowed. "I guess."

"Good. I knew you were a real Aquarius."

The column slowed and stopped. Frank peered ahead, waiting. In the dark it was hard to make anything out. Then he saw the trees.

"The park?" He raised his eyebrows. " 'Save Sunrise Park'?"

"You figured it out, congratulations." He felt her anger through the dark. " 'Sunrise Parking Lot,' for God's sake! Listen, if we can stop the bastards here, or even slow them down . . ."

Sigrid was gesturing. They crept ahead in a crouch, crossing the street. Kent was working the wire cutter. In a moment a piece of the chain-link fence fell forward. One by one they moved through the hole. The enemy loomed up in the dark: bulldozers, giant caterpillars, dump trucks.

The five shadows assembled and distributed the tools. "He knows diesels, he can work with me," Frieda muttered. "Give him a wrench and a wire cutter."

They fanned out, Frank and Frieda together. "Go for the radiators and fuel injector pumps, they're easiest." She yanked open the hood of a dump truck and tugged furiously at cables and hoses for a minute, making instant spaghetti of the motor, then located the injector pump with her pocket flashlight and took Frank's wrench, like a surgeon selecting an instrument. The working end of the wrench was wrapped in a white sock. She swung it hard into the pump. There was a soft *thunk* and a tinkle. She did it again. And again. Frank shivered.

"Now the radiator. Your job." She started him off, jamming the wire cutter in, with the jaws around a copper tube. Frank took the handle, but as he started to cut, he found himself paralyzed. He thought of his beautiful Stingray and all of his old cars, the Rabbit, the Impala, his father's vintage Bearcat. Like killing a child. He couldn't do it.

"What are you waiting for?"

"I—just—can't."

"What do you mean, you can't? You're an Aquarius, aren't you? Take a deep breath, damn it!"

He sucked in smog and choked, and in the spasms of coughing, his hands gripped into fists, and under the steel-handled cutter he felt a soft yielding, heard liquid trickling, a thin moaning from the wounded radiator. Aroused, he located another tube and squeezed again.

"First blood," she whispered. "Now you're really one of us."

They moved along, from 'dozer to cat to dump truck, working hard, hearing muffled *thunks* from other places nearby. Somewhere a dog barked and another one answered. Frank went rigid, but the barking soon stopped. They passed close by Kent, who was funneling sugar into a gas tank. Frieda whispered something to him, and Frank heard his easy laugh.

Minutes passed. Frieda yanked out cables and killed injector pumps while Frank butchered radiators. They stepped up the pace, five minutes per vehicle. Frank began to feel righteous, a crusader striking down heathen.

Frieda's anger seemed to be swelling as they went on. She attacked a big dump truck with a low snarl, tearing at cables, smashing fuel injectors, cutting through radiator hoses and fan belts. "Bastards," she hissed. "Bastards!"

Frank watched her in awe, pausing over the dribbling radiator. "Here, help me with this alternator."

He pulled a filter aside, and Frieda's wrench crashed into the alternator, sending metal flying.

"Take it easy. You'll lose an eye or something."

"Too many of them! Too few of us!" She battered the oil pump. "Environmental Resistance Groups—outnumbered a thousand to one." She knocked out the oil filter, wrecked the fuse box, spit on the dead engine, and jumped down off the mutilated truck.

"You don't have to do it all yourself."

"Who the hell else is there? Somebody's got to save the world, right?"

He smiled: her little joke again. But she was going on angrily.

"Will the real estate millionaires do it?" She pulled an ice pick out of her boot and thrust it deftly into the sidewall of a big tire, slipping it out again to a soft sighing sound. Twice more, then to another tire. Again, again. The air was full of soughing breezes. "Will the news-papers help? The politicians? The schools? And the churches—the churches are skimming off the gravy, birthrights for pottage, money changers in the temples. The system, oh God, the system!" She stabbed the fourth tire, a furious thrust, and sank to her knees, face in her greasy hands. Frank thought she must be crying, weeping away her outrage. He put a hand on her shoulder, but she sprang up immediately and turned her pocket flashlight onto her wrist.

"Time's up." She whistled twice, a birdlike warble, and answering whistles sang through the dark. "No matter how much good you're doing, you've got to get in and out in half an hour. Live to fight another day. Scramble!"

Silhouettes sifted through the dark, scurrying for the hole in the fence.

"So far we've been lucky," she said, trudging the alleyways back to the garage. "No arrests."

After the excitement, Frank was beginning to feel let down and repentant. "But is it worth it? The risk? You may not be lucky forever."

"Don't have to be lucky forever. Or anything else forever. All we have to do is cripple the system a little, here today, there tomorrow, somewhere else the next day. Make it expensive for them. And slow."

"But fighting the system—it's always a losing battle. Isn't it?"

"The park isn't dead yet. And the big nuke on the river's a year behind schedule, and looks more like a turkey every day."

Frank was troubled, the angst of an apostate, lover of engines, worshiper of chrome and high velocities. "Still," he persisted, "all this destruction of good machines, doesn't it bother you?"

"Wasting anything bothers me. But wasting the wasters, that's different. Listen, we weren't always like this. We started out with petitions and peaceful marches. Even court orders. Injunctions. But nothing stopped them for long. So when they started ripping out the trees, we came in one night with a flatbed truck, and for every tree they'd uprooted, we planted three healthy saplings, good strong twenty-footers, ash, maple, birch, redbud, dogwood. We worked all night." She sighed. "The next day they bulldozed them all down, of course."

She walked on a few yards before she said anything else, and when she spoke, her anger was back. "It's always the people who never get involved, who sit on the sidelines and don't help, they're always the ones who criticize when we're finally forced to go underground, isn't that so?" He could feel her glaring at him. "God, if I didn't know you were an Aquarius, sometimes I'd swear you were a Pisces."

Against his better judgment, Frank felt vaguely insulted.

In a moment her seventeen-year-old mood had changed, and she took his hand. "Come on, confess, you enjoyed it, didn't you? Saving the world? Playing God? You loved it."

The delicious surge in his chest: he found himself whistling Frieda's little bird-warble.

But his happiness, always perishable, didn't last. An hour later, tossing in his rumpled bed, he was sweating pure guilt again.

THIRTEEN

ELECTION DAY dawn filtered its way to the Steak and Lobster Inn, where Frank lay awake, listening to the muted thump of pacing in the next room. Julian had been with Fat Mama until very late, and something must have been preying on him since. Twice Frank had heard him pad outside to the candy machine, drop many coins, and pull levers. Julian's brain food: by now surely he should have figured it out, whatever was troubling him.

But whatever it was, Frank absolutely refused to let himself be interested, to get mousetrapped again. His phony beard itched. He hadn't washed his face for two days, scared to be without his flimsy disguise even in bed. A matter of life and death.

Frank thought of the tea party and felt his legs sticking to the clammy sheets. He dreaded the feeble sun, now probing its way between the two steep eastern crags and through his half-open curtains. He hadn't slept much, either, and his snatches of sleep had been fidgety with nightmares.

Without warning or ceremony Julian burst through the door of the adjoining rooms, munching a Milky Way and carrying one of his massive scholarly volumes. He was talking before he got into the room.

". . . thinking Freyr, Freyr, Freyr, just because there are some unaccountable runes around this kooky county, not to mention a Viking ship complete with a chained skeleton. But there are a basketful of sun-gods, after all. What about Ra, what about Indra, what about Apollo, what about Mithra?"

"What about getting the hell out of my room and coming back when it's daylight, and maybe even knocking?" Frank rolled over in bed. "I mean, if you've got to talk sun-gods, you might have the decency to wait till the sun's up."

"The sun is up, look at it." Julian bolted the rest of his Milky Way and opened the curtains wider. He stared for a moment, pensive, at the red mass lumbering into the purple smudge of the sky. "The unconquered sun, a fifth-rate star, off at the edge of the galaxy, sacred in a hundred lands, by a hundred names. So why just Freyr? All this Oriental clutter, Mithra, the mysteries, maybe it's real, maybe it's not just a hoax or a curiosity, maybe it's right at the center of this mess. And that's why we're not getting anywhere with Wong and the Vikings."

Frank pulled the covers over his head.

Julian paced the room, sending tremors through faults in the flooring. "Vespasian had three legions along the Euphrates, Trajan founded a colony at Nineveh, and then Hadrian pulls Asian troops, all of them worshipers of Mithra, into the defense of the European frontiers, the *Limes*. Connections? My God, just think of the connections, foot soldiers from Commagene and Cappadocia along the northern outposts, squadrons of Parthian cavalry, auxiliary troops from all over the East."

Frank felt himself getting interested again, caught up, against his will, in Julian's preposterous Vikings. He threw off the covers. "Julian, I'm getting out."

Julian plunked the big book on the bed, talking fast. "Look here, it was standard imperial policy to use the barbarian auxiliaries as far from their homes as possible, to prevent uprisings. So just think of the comings and goings, the administrators, the officers, the turnover in personnel! And Roman soldiers were just about the most superstitious louts who ever carried spears, pious, even. I mean, when you're out there on the prickly frontiers of nowhere, with the arrows zinging in from who knows which direction, you want to be damn sure the gods are on your side, right? Long before Constantine, Frank, long before Constantine staged his glorious butchery under the sign of the cross, it was Mithra who really mattered to our ancestors, who spread his cult across the face of Europe. Except for that one battle of Constantine's, you and I might be prostrating ourselves to Mithra, in some underground Mithreum, this very day."

"I said I'm getting the hell out of here." Frank was out of bed, pulling on his pants. Julian went back to the window.

"But the clincher is the *Limes*. The Eighth Legion, transferred from Moesia to Germany, the Fifteenth sent north to the Danube, then the Twelfth, the Thirtieth. By the time of the Antonines it was all there, every ingredient, all provided for. The unconquered sun!"

Frank tugged him away from the window and closed the curtains again. "Listen for a minute, will you? I've been thinking about this all night. I'm really leaving this time. Today. And I'm taking Frieda with me, if she'll go. Do you hear me?"

There was a pause. The familiar snarl and murmur of traffic. Julian concentrated on Frank with what seemed an enormous effort. "Leaving?"

"I'm not interested in Wong and his Vikings, not the least little bit. Also, we're sitting around here eating too damn much. Also, this mangy beard itches. Also, half the people in this town want me dead, and I'm scared. I don't know what the others want from me, but it's something unhealthy. Also, the air conditioning is half-ass, we're losing money every day, we'll go broke out here in the boonies, and all you can talk about is the sun. Why didn't you go to Florida?"

Julian turned away, opened the curtains again, and stood there thoughtfully. "I remember what your daddy used to say. Never get off a plane before it's on the ground, he'd say."

Frank began to feel the reassuring warmth, seduced by the aphorism before he knew what it implied. But he shook it off: none of that.

"By which he meant, don't pull out of Ash Garden till you've done what you came to do."

"He meant no such thing. He meant don't go tomfooling in the haystacks, when there's a pile of work to be done right at home in good old New York, that's what he meant. When you're fleecing a willing lamb, don't waste your time looking for goats, that's what he said." Frank felt better, stronger. He was leaving, leaving Ash Garden.

"He was a smart man. He made some mistakes, sure, but one thing he never did was paint himself into a corner. On your way in, look for the exits, that's what he always said. New York's a dead end for us."

"Dead end? With all this new elitism around? High schools wanting teachers with doctorates now, and more and more phonies and incompetents coming up for their Ed.D.'s every year, and Confidential Services, Inc., in line for a killing? You call that a dead end? Remember what else my father said—give people what they need, you'll make a living. Give them what they want, you'll make a fortune."

"Your daddy said it right when he said, a dead end is when a racket looks as good to the hoods and the cops as it does to the management. The business is too good, Frank. They're after a piece of it. He always said, go far enough into debt and your creditor is your partner. Make a big enough profit and the government is your partner. We've got a pretty good stake now, enough to do as we please for a while, go where we want to, relax. He always said, it's not too smart to fight fire with fire, when you've got matches and they've got flame throwers."

Barely 7 A.M. and Frank was already so weary he had to sit down. All that easy money, just waiting for quick dissertations—lost, lost. "I'm not going to argue with you any more, but I'll be damned if I'm staying in this nutty town one more day."

"Yes, just one more day. Our girl friends are foisting the wrong cave on us, doesn't that gall you? And things are moving now. The election's today. Maybe it'll clear up some mysteries around here. Maybe it'll even clear up J. Randolph Wong."

"But why? One good reason."

"For the truth, son. After four years of incessant, professional lying, the truth at last." He sounded ecstatic and a little crazy, like a TV evangelist.

Frank snickered. "The truth is for the second set of books, my father used to say."

Julian went to the window again. "Sooner or later, there's a moment of truth that really looks like the truth." He nodded. "You know who said that? Your daddy said it. The last time I ever saw him alive."

Julian cleared his throat. "Come on, let's wake somebody up and get breakfast. And then take a little walk and see if we spot any Szechwan restaurants or hand laundries in the neighborhood."

FOURTEEN

THEY DIDN'T HAVE to wake anybody up. Frieda and Fat Mama were already serving a dozen early voters. Frieda came over to their booth, walking with that familiar awkwardness so much lovelier than grace, so timeless that he always felt like falling on his knees to her.

Instead, she bent over him, patting his beard. "Not bad, after that hard night's work. A little brushing here and there, and you'll be ready to face the world." She poured coffee. "Same as yesterday, Julian?"

He nodded and drank off the cup in one tilt, like a shot of red-eye. She poured him another. "Frank?"

"Two over light, and toast. And happy birthday." He sipped the coffee. Superb, as always. "My compliments to the chef."

"Thank you, our pleasure." Her half-smile mocked him as she slipped off to the kitchen.

Later, when Julian was finishing his morning feast, Fat Mama pulled up a chair.

"Nice to see you putting away those sausages, Capricorn. Think positively." She winked and elbowed him in the ribs.

Julian assumed an elegant posture. "We're on the point of stepping forth into the world, to watch the electioneering and get a breath of your fresh country air."

"Still after your mysterious Chinaman?" Fat Mama laughed and looked outside. "Well, the weather seems OK. Be prepared for changes today."

"May we have the pleasure of your company on our little stroll?"

She thought it over. "Oh, why the hell not? I have to vote anyway, and things are under control here. The drinking crowd won't be coming in till about noon. I'll tell the kitchen."

Frank resisted. "I don't think I want to be seen in the streets."

"Don't be chicken," Julian chided. "I'm telling you, nobody's going to get hurt, this is all just a PG thriller."

"You'll be all right with me, Gemini, don't worry." It was an order.

So the two bulky people, arm in arm, swept down the crowded sidewalk, clearing a path, and in the void behind them, Frank and Frieda strolled through a summer love of their own, hardly noticing the constant billboards.

VOTE FOR MAGNUS—CRUSH BIG OLAF

RE-ELECT BIG OLAF—MURDER MAGNUS

VOTE FOR MAGNUS—SLAUGHTER BIG OLAF

RE-ELECT BIG OLAF—MASSACRE MAGNUS

Campaign cars cruised the streets, their sides covered with photos of the candidates, loudspeakers crackling out catchy college fight songs, military marches, and campaign rhetoric, conjuring the church of a thousand years of order, conjuring the thousand-horsepower car.

When the moment seemed right, Frank worked up his courage. "Frieda, I've got to get out of this town. Soon. Will you go with me?"

He was afraid she'd ask where, but she only glanced at him, sideways. "Maybe, Aquarius. Try me again later. Afterward."

After what? Well, it was a chance. Her little bird-warble sang in his head.

The air of holiday was infectious. Hot dog and ice cream vendors clanged and shouted. Shopping centers were doing a brisk business.

At the curbings, teenagers knelt by their gleaming Skylarks and Wildcats and Cobras, reverently polishing them, or sat behind the wheel with the driver's door open, blaring their horns at friends in the crowd. Most of the cars had bumper stickers.

FREE MEN OWN GUNS
SLAVES DON'T

The polling places were busy, the bullhorn electioneering at the doors deafening. Fat Mama, her civic duty done, emerged from a booth looking smug. Frank squeezed Frieda's hand. It was his last day in Ash Garden.

The morning passed pleasantly, with much evidence of Olaf and Magnus, but not a hint of J. Randolph Wong or anything remotely Oriental. Julian began getting grumpy, so at noon Fat Mama led them back to the Steak and Lobster Inn and regaled them with a birthday banquet that was irresistibly delicious and stupefying in its magnitude. But Fat Mama was acting strangely nervous, and Frieda only picked at her food, looking preoccupied. She seemed uninterested in her cake, blazing with eighteen candles. Frank and Julian atoned for this delinquency, eating and drinking for two solid hours, before stumbling off to bed to rest up for dinner.

FIFTEEN

FRANK woke with a headache. He fumbled his way to the bathroom and found aspirins. The tap water was frothy as usual and tasted like half-and-half chlorine, but it gave him a virtuous feeling, swallowing the pills.

Waiting for relief, he realized that he was not hearing any of the sounds a civilized person always expects to hear: no cars, no motorcycles, no sirens. The silence was spooky.

He groped his way to the window. The smog was creating an artificial dusk, like an eclipse. The twin hilltops in the east were pink-gold and indistinct. Fat Mama's neon sign flashed red through the murk.

The streets were empty. In the parking lot with his Stingray there were only two other cars, a Spider and a Scorpion, bearing the same bumper sticker.

GUNS DON'T KILL PEOPLE
PEOPLE KILL PEOPLE

Frank tightened the muscles in his squeamish stomach and crossed to Julian's door. At the third knock, Julian finally said something indistinguishable, and Frank entered. He went first to the bathroom for a glass, then to Julian's bed, carrying the aspirin bottle and water. He shook the bulky form. Julian rolled, a great whale ready to sound. Finally he opened his eyes and saw the aspirin.

"Thank God." He swallowed half a dozen of them. "Damn these morning-afters."

"It's not morning, it's evening. And there's something funny going on. Come look out the window."

Julian groaned, grumbled, got up, and lurched to the window. He stared. "Vacuumed away." He studied for a moment. "Well, let's find out what's what."

When they got to the restaurant, it was deserted except for Frieda and Fat Mama. "Hi, there, sleepyheads. Happy hour, have a bowl of mead, on the house." Frank was surprised. She seemed drunk. Sotted, in fact: her huge bulk weaved through the empty tables perilously, a scow in heavy seas. "Be ready for anything today, fellows. Lunar aspect favors change. Come watch the returns."

The television screen was showing Ash Garden Election Central, the big board covered with precinct grids, still blank. An announcer was baring her teeth in professional excitement. Fat Mama tried to adjust the color; the screen oozed red like an abrasion. "Just a minute or two now and we ought to know," she boomed out, slurring her words badly. "Polls close at six."

Frank had to ask. "Fat Mama, why isn't there anybody here? Or out on the streets?"

She stared at him. "Nobody, Gemini? Still? Nobody at all?" She plopped down in a chair, and it squeaked and skidded a little. Julian sat down beside her, and she gave him a trembling hand, but wouldn't look at him, her eyes on the big screen. Besides being drunk, Frank realized, she was remarkably nervous.

The crowd at Election Central was in two groups, a younger set, obviously Olaf's supporters, waving red flowers like pom-pom girls, and the middle-aged crew with their Legion uniforms, Magnus pennants, and gun belts.

Frieda brought bowls of mead, the tray shaking. "Why aren't there any people outside?" Frank asked her.

She gave him that ambiguous sidelong glance. "Well, we're not sure. Except that it may be dangerous tonight. We've heard so many rumors . . ."

There was a time signal on the television.

"Six o'clock," the announcer said. "The polls are closed. And now we switch to our computer analysts, to bring you the results of this hard-fought battle between the incumbent sheriff, Big Olaf, and his vigorous challenger, Father Magnus. Gentlemen?"

The screen blipped and produced a vision of computer hardware at work. Two men in white jackets were watching green numbers flash across monitors. They conferred for a moment and then nodded decisively.

"Thank you, Hilda," one of them said. "Well, with the polls now closed, the results are feeding directly from the voting machines into our computers at Election Central. We've examined our sample precincts, and there's no question about the outcome. With ten percent of the votes already in, it's clear that the winner, with a final total of fifty-six percent, will be Father Magnus."

Fat Mama drank off her bowl of mead without a word. Frieda was kneeling by Frank's chair, holding his fingers in her cold hands. Staring at the television, she hardly seemed aware of him at all.

The picture dissolved to Election Central, where the grinning announcer was trying to make herself heard above bedlam. Magnus's veterans had pulled out pistols and were firing in the air. Olaf's young supporters were scattering for the exits.

"There you have it," the announcer crowed, "a clear victory for Father Magnus, who will be the new sheriff of . . ."

The firing drowned her out, and now Magnus's men were no

longer firing in the air but directly at the fleeing young people. A curly-haired boy pitched forward as if he'd been tripped. Julian choked, spewing mead.

The camera zoomed in on a tall blond girl as several slugs caught her in the back, twisting her one way, then another. Frank blinked, not believing his eyes. Her body turned in slow motion, and he gasped. It looked like Sigrid. A red flower dropped from her hand, and she slid to the floor like a balloon losing air.

One of the legionnaires pointed a gun at the camera. The screen went gray.

Frank flinched; Frieda's fingernails were digging into his palm. She was staring at the dead television, her mouth half open. She seemed to have stopped breathing.

The video came back on, showing an old movie. Fat Mama tried another channel: a game show. She slammed the Off button. "Sons of bitches!" she exploded. "Now they've gone and done it!" She poured herself another bowl of mead and drank it fast, then poured another.

Julian's voice was hoarse. "What the hell's going on?" He was gasping and wheezing, as if he were having an attack.

Gunfire rattled in the street. Shadowy figures darted past the restaurant windows, and Frank caught glimpses of the Legion uniforms. Frieda's hands were squeezing his, as cold as death.

"I don't know, Capricorn, it's all got out of hand. All those rumors, it's not like the good old days . . ." She waddled to the front door and locked it, then flipped all the Venetian blinds shut.

The popping of guns outside became a steady roll, like automatic rifles. There were screams close by. Frank rubbed Frieda's cold hands gently. She wouldn't look at him, just sat there, frozen in place.

Julian persisted, his voice shrill with disbelief. "What rumors? What are you talking about? Why is that shoot-out going on out there? Say something, Sybil!"

She glared back at him defiantly, as if she'd been cornered. "I tell you I don't know. It's all different, they're not following the rules, it's everyone for himself now."

There was a crash at the front door, so loud that Frank thought the glass must have broken. Fat Mama backed away as if something were threatening her. Nobody else moved. Reluctantly Frank eased out of Frieda's grip, edged over to the door, and pulled up the blind.

Frieda screamed, a long crescendo of pain. Kent was lying in the doorway, his head against the glass door, eyes open and staring, his face mashed into a flat parody of itself.

Still screaming, Frieda ran to the door and tried to shove it open, but the inert body held it shut. Frank put his shoulder to the door and heaved as hard as he could, forcing it open little by little. Wedging herself through the opening, Frieda took Kent in her arms, crying his name. Finally Frank got through the doorway, carried Kent into the restaurant, and laid him on the floor. Frieda crawled beside him and cradled his head in her lap.

"Call an ambulance!" Frank yelled. "A doctor!" In a frenzy, he tore off Kent's shirt, but the wound was farther down, the torn trousers, the blood. When he opened the pants, he gasped: not a neat flesh wound but the appalling gash of a dumdum, the red flow getting weaker. No case for first aid. Nothing to be done. "A doctor!" he called again, his voice gone feeble. He knew it was too late. He covered the wound and knelt there.

Fat Mama was on the phone, trying to call the ambulance service, doctors, the sheriff. But no one answered, anywhere. "Son of a bitch!" she kept howling. "Son of a bitch!"

Julian hobbled over to Kent and went through the motions: no pulse, no breath.

"Frieda," Julian murmured. "I'll take care of him."

She didn't answer.

Julian tried to release her hold on Kent. He tugged gently at her. "You'd better help me, Frank."

Together they worked at the cold fingers, loosening the incredibly hard grip. Julian lifted Kent awkwardly and staggered away to a back room.

Frieda remained where she was, silent, seeing nothing. Frank put an arm around her. "Frieda. Frieda. It's all over."

But guns hammered again in the street. Fat Mama knelt and warmed the girl's hands in hers. "Frieda, my baby, I'm here , you'll be all right." She took the slight figure in her arms, blond head on the great pillow of her bosom, and rocked her gently.

Julian came back, looking bewildered and very tired. Fat Mama explained. "We told Kent to come here if there was trouble." Her voice went fuzzy, and she cleared her throat. "He almost made it."

She rocked Frieda like an infant. Her voice sang on, a boozy lullaby, "I love you, baby, forget." She stroked Frieda's hair, rubbed her arms. Slowly the girl regained herself.

Fat Mama looked relieved. "She's coming back." She sounded rueful: "I don't know what to tell you, Capricorn. The elections are getting worse all the time. It used to be just the hunt for the losing candidate, the way it's always been, our local tradition, ageless. But then came the spying, the dirty tricks, bugging, break-ins, then abductions and assassinations. Now everyone's paying the big price, the leaders, precinct captains, party workers, activists. Madness! So this is his church of a thousand years of order. Oh, God!"

Julian listened with narrowed eyes.

Frank held Frieda's cold hands. "My gentle Aquarius," she repeated, her voice coming from a far-off place, toneless, mechanical.

SIXTEEN

TWO HOURS later it was nearly dark, a gray drizzle cutting off the evening light. The mead had done its job, and the four of them sat there numb in the presence of death, a vigil. Frieda was crying softly, mourning her friends, her lost cadre. The shooting outside was intermittent and far off.

Julian, his feet propped on a chair, was leaning back, talking steadily, a long lamentation for atrocities: "Eyewitnesses all agreed, there were whirlwinds and phantom lights. Fire dragons flew through the air, and the merciless Viking heathen laid waste the Church of God in Lindisfarne, with plundering and killing. The words of Jeremiah shamed the ears of sinners, 'Out of the North an evil shall break forth on all the inhabitants of the land.'

"And later on, the holy shrines of Jarrow and Monkswearmouth weltered in pious blood. No harbor, no stronghold, no fortress in Europe was free from the Viking peril, the square-rigged sails and dragon prows looming out of the mist, hell-bent for plunder, slaves, and blood. Six hundred long ships on the Elbe destroyed Hamburg, a hundred ships on the Seine besieged Paris, wrecking the army of

Charles the Bald, stringing up a host of French troops like old laundry, food for crows, sacrifice to Wodan. Human sacrifice."

Frank held the small rough hands that wouldn't warm, and whispered, "Come with me now, away from this." Then he said it for the second time, and this time he knew what he was doing. "I love you." It was something entirely new in his life.

And at last his mother's voice came through to him, a gentle singsong: *to be good*, it was saying.

Frieda's wet eyes were a blue to drown in. "Anywhere, away from here, anywhere, my gentle Aquarius."

No, not Aquarius, no more illusions. Say, instead, I'll go with you anywhere for your own sake, for our sake. That's the way it is, the way it must be—*to be good*—no father's crafty cynicism, no moralizing stars to shine in one night sky or another, only the two of us together. Alone, together.

But Frieda was too pale for all that now. Julian's cadence continued.

" 'And Jephthah, Judge of Israel, destroyer of Ammon, vowed a vow unto the Lord, and said, whatsoever cometh forth of the doors of my house to meet me, shall surely be the Lord's, and I will offer it up for a burnt offering.

" 'And behold, his daughter came out to meet him, and she was his only child, and he rent his clothes, and he said Alas, for I have opened my mouth to the Lord, and I cannot go back.

" 'And he did with her according to his vow, which he had vowed.' "

The thousand cynical gospels learned at his father's knee. Frank felt it all fading, the hand-me-down fit of his father's shoddy creed, the grim exploitation of truth: overcome, surmounted at last, he was sure now. *To be good.* He whispered love to Frieda.

Julian's tempo slowed. "And if children were also expendable in the great temple at Uppsala, if young girls were sacrificed to Freyr on Midsummer Day, why not . . ."

He paused. Rifle fire sputtered in the distance.

"Why not in Asgard?"

SEVENTEEN

ASGARD, Ash Garden, mumbo jumbo. The time had come. "Julian," Frank said. "Fat Mama."

They listened, big eyed and hushed as if at a sickbed.

"Frieda and I. We want to tell you. We're going away. Tonight."

That feeling of a trap closing on him. Where was it now?

Julian looked worried. Fat Mama spoke. "But baby, you know what's out there."

Frieda shuddered and sipped at her mead. Frank was done with it all. "Don't scare her any more."

"Some fears are healthy, Gemini. Be cautious today." She paused as if making a decision, then went on. "Magnus is out there, with all his legionnaires. They're leading a black bull through the streets, our oldest custom. They're hunting for Olaf."

"And if they find him?"

"*When* they find him," she corrected him. "When they find him, he'll be taken to the altar, and—well, you know." She put a hand on Frieda's forehead. "It's too damn dangerous, baby. Too dangerous to go anywhere now." She glared at Frank. "Don't you understand, they're still after you, too. If they see you bolt, they'll get you, sure as hell. Tell him, Frieda."

Frieda was as gray as limestone, her voice a whisper. "I'm going with him."

Fat Mama made a sound like a sob.

Julian cleared his throat. "He wouldn't go out there now. He wouldn't think of leaving now, at night, with those trigger-happy cretins tracking him like a possum."

Abruptly, rifles crackled in the street nearby.

"That's just it. They're closing in. Sooner or later, they'll grab me, and that'll be that. So we're going."

"But where? What are your plans?"

"No plans. I've got enough money for a while. And there'll be some other kind of work, somewhere. Anyway, you don't need me any more. You don't need me for your truth, your honesty."

"You mean you don't need me any more." Julian looked somber.

Frieda gazed at Frank. He had never felt so strong.

"So you're both sure?"

Frieda managed a smile. "This minute. Now." But her voice was shaky.

Fat Mama was crying. She kissed Frieda. "Oh, baby, be happy. Plan the future wisely. Live in the present." She snuffled. "I'm happy for you, happy. And for you, too, Gemini, you frigging daughter thief. Congratulations."

"Thank you, Mama." Frieda frowned. "But he's not a Gemini, it hurts me to hear you keep calling him that. He's an Aquarius, my own gentle Aquarius."

Frank nodded. Fat Mama was astonished.

"A perfectly understandable error," Julian smiled, "since Frank lied to you—that is, misled you, about both of us. But the fact is, it doesn't matter, because apparently Frank doesn't really know his own sign, either. I guess I'm the only one who knows it, now that his daddy's gone."

The chitchat was making Frank impatient. "Don't confuse things. For what it's worth, Fat Mama, I'm an Aquarius."

"It's worth everything." Frieda's voice was still shaky. Frank stared at her, troubled. She looked down, avoiding his eyes.

"I'm afraid not," Julian interposed. "He's neither a Gemini nor an Aquarius."

"But he told me . . ."

"Frank's horoscope is clear enough, Frieda. He was born on February nineteenth."

"Well, then."

"A cusp day. Only the beginning of it's Aquarian. And Frank was born in the evening. It's in the medical records, public information. He's a Pisces."

Gunfire erupted in the street, and bullets crashed through the plate glass window of the restaurant. Everyone dropped to the floor, Fat Mama yelling in anger.

On her knees, Frieda turned to him, her eyes gone curiously blank, as if nobody lived behind them. "Is that true, Frank? A Pisces?" It was a voice he had never heard before. Something had altered the universe.

Frank was confused. "Well, I don't know. I mean, I've always thought I was an Aquarius, not that it ever mattered. But if Julian says . . ."

Guns hammered in the street again, and stray bullets smashed into the bar and the television. Broken glass spewed in all directions. Everyone ducked, and Fat Mama banged her fist on the floor.

Frieda stared at him. "Then it's true?" Her anger was back again. Frank crawled over to her and tried to take her hands, but she pulled back from him as from a slimy thing.

"Not an Aquarius? A *Pisces?* All that—what I thought was a generous, understanding Aquarius, is really only a wishy-washy Pisces?"

Frank tried to be patient. "Don't you see, it doesn't really matter."

"That warm Aquarian affection, really only Pisces jealousy? That Aquarian independence, only Pisces moodiness?"

Fat Mama was alternately nodding along with her and shaking her head accusingly at Frank. On her knees, she put an arm around Frieda, protectively.

"Frieda, will you stop it?" Frank realized he was shouting. "Listen, you're still upset from all the shooting, the killing, you're not your-self, you're delirious, and you're drunk, and you're talking a lot of superstitious poppycock. Can't you hear how silly it sounds?"

She sucked in air as though he had struck her. Rage quivered in her neck muscles. She was losing all control. Frank wanted to take back everything he'd just said, to grab her, hold her tight. "Frieda!"

"Hypocrisy! Fraud! Men! Oh, *men!*" Her eyes glinted, not seeing him, not looking at him. "No wonder you lied to Mama."

"I didn't lie, exactly. It was an innocent little joke." But guilt, sneaking up unexpectedly, got a hand on his throat.

"That's just the way a Pisces talks! I see it now. Thank the stars I found out in time. You're just like the others."

Frank shouted, "What difference does it make if I was born in the morning or the evening? Whoever I was five minutes ago, I still am! Nobody changes like that!" He grabbed her wrist. She twisted out of his grasp and rubbed her arm ruefully, as if he had savaged it.

"You are what you are!" she cried. "I didn't make you one thing or the other, the stars do that. But at last I see what you really are, a Pisces bully!"

"Frieda, I love you!"

But it was too late. She was running out of the room, her low wail keening down the hallway. "Men!"

"You can't mean it!" he shouted after her. "It's insane!"

"Really, I ought to take offense," Fat Mama muttered. "But I only feel sorry for you, Pisces." She followed Frieda.

Julian spoke, apologetic. "I don't know what to say. I had no idea she'd take it like that."

"Are you sure you had no idea?"

"On my honor. Astrology's just a tabloid amusement, after all, a harmless little game."

"And what matters is whether you win or lose," Frank added bitterly. Harmless? Why, when he was so clearly right, did they all make him feel like a naughty schoolboy, always wrong, wrong, wrong? Klutz! Jessie's Bronx voice screamed in his head.

To be good.

Nice guys finish last.

Pouring himself a bowl of mead, he held it high in salute: "Happy birthday, Frieda."

In the silence, rifles yammered again, farther away now. The trap had sprung, grabbing him in its saw-toothed grip, the pain in his ragged nerves piercing disbelief, scattering numbness, leaving him alone with his sudden, useless tears.

EIGHTEEN

JULIAN led Frank back to their rooms. He turned the key, but the door wasn't locked. When he pushed it open, they both gasped. The place had been ripped apart. Bedding was everywhere, clothes flung in heaps, books scattered around the floor. The adjoining room was a wreck.

Julian was poking around in the debris. "Systematic. But not vandalism."

"How the hell do you define vandalism?"

"Well, look around. No picture tubes shattered, no slashed furniture."

"OK, OK, I get it, we're lucky, right? Fortune's children." Frank was too desolate to care. Frieda, Frieda . . .

"All I mean is that this wasn't a grudge. It was a hunt, a furious hunt. And for what? I give you one guess."

"Don't tell me. Wong's crazy manuscript?"

"You put your finger on it, son. And so did they. Parchments, translations, all gone. And as far as I can tell, they're the only things missing."

"But who did it? Why?"

"Wouldn't we like to know. Olaf? Magnus? Wong himself, whoever he is? Or somebody else, someone we least suspect? They obviously know who *we* are, and they're only putting up with us in the hope that we'll lead them to something. To gold, maybe? Well, I'll tell you this. With all those new translations in their hands, they're about as close to the answer as I am. Which means there's not much time left." Julian was agitated, pacing the littered floor.

"But there's something they haven't got," he added, pulling some wrinkled papers out of his shirt pocket. "These are what they went to all this trouble for, and without them I doubt if they'll be able to figure out the rest of it. I haven't figured it out myself, for that matter, but I will. I will, by God, if I have to stay up all the rest of this night. They're not going to take me by surprise again, and I'm not quitting until I've got what I came for."

He turned to Frank and sighed. "Look, you're bushed, you've had a bad day. Go in there and pull a blanket out of that mess and get some sleep. Our time here may be running out, but as long as we've got these, we're still safe." He thought a minute. "Or anyway, we should be safe."

NINETEEN

MOURNING his losses, too upset to be sleepy, Frank tore off his clothes, threw himself onto the bed, pulled the tangled sheets around him, and tossed and floundered, and saw his father's body dangling from the terrace, and turned over and heard gunfire, and flopped again in the damp sheets and thought about Frieda, and found himself in his father's apartment, which blurred into someone else's apartment, and he was on the floor, and Jessie Bell, the biggest, toughest girl in the ninth grade, hockey player, team wrestler, street fighter, bigger than all the freshman boys, held him in a hammerlock, and had his belt unbuckled, and he sat straight up in bed with his eyes open and swore he would not let himself think about that again; and he heard Julian working the balky candy machine in the hall, muttering curses, and he wasn't really asleep and he wasn't really awake, and he was in the strange apartment again, and his arm hurt, and she had his fly unzipped and was working his pants down, tug by tug, irresistible, and he was squirming in fear and shame, pulling feebly against her terrible hammerlock and moaning at the pain of it, sharp stabbings in his shoulder and back.

"Come on, baby," she was cooing, "you've been waiting for this since the seventh grade." He bent his legs to hold his pants up. "Let go, Frankie." She gave his arm a sharp thrust, and white pain glimmered behind his eyes. His legs straightened, the pants were kicked down and off, she did it with her toes, never letting up on the tight hammerlock.

Then his shorts, too, and he was bare on the prickly rug in her parents' deserted apartment where he never should have come with her, outweighed by a good thirty pounds of her Girls' Athletic Association muscle, his own skinny arms still clinging to Little League.

He sat up in bed, furious. He would not think about that again, a grown man, twenty-four years old, with a steady job, adult responsibilities, a rich and varied sex life, a whole range of mature relationships extending all the way from lingering handshakes to party kisses to long weekends in the Hamptons, he simply would not lie on a vandalized motel bed, would not lie there in sweaty, twisted sheets and listen to a teen-age bully clucking at his back, her buttery double-feature popcorn breath wafting over his shoulder, "You're so pretty, little Frankie," her free hand stroking his thighs, fondling his testicles as he twitched at her touching.

And then she was holding his penis, and agony cramped his chest: *to be good.* He screamed for help in the empty apartment, a howl of the heart. She kicked him, sharp hockey-playing knee fierce in the spine, a flash of fire in his back. He sucked in air to scream again, but could only gasp, his breath coming in a strange wheezing rush.

"Yell again, you little putz, and I'll kick the living shit out of you." She sounded exactly like her father, the Giants' linebacker. "What are you so scared of, a little fooling around?"

"Please, Jessie!" He recognized his own whisper, the prayers of all his fourteen years: "I don't want to."

She gave his arm a yank. She was tough, the meanest wrestler on the girl's junior varsity, he shouldn't have come here, she was relentless, her right hand caressing his testicles again, slowly moving to his scared penis, gently working the limp thing back and forth, back and forth, patience. "You're so cute, so soft and skinny all over, I get all gooey in my pants when you answer Mr. Howell's questions. Come on, get it hard for me, rise and shine."

"You're hurting my arm. Please, you've got to believe me, I've never—I've never done . . ." The hammerlock tightened and his voice limped off into a whimper.

"I know, that's just it, I want your cherry. You want this, too, you just don't know it yet. But you'll thank me for it later."

Her fingers played skillfully with his penis, and he felt a sickening dread in his heart: it was getting hard. He fought it with all his soul, he tried to think of his mother, of Mr. Howell, but nothing would stop it now, her fingers toying with him, gently working it back and forth, back and forth, back and forth. It was getting rock-hard, no escape, and he was wild with desire and fear, and he felt her body slide on top of him, flat on his back now, his arm beneath him almost numb with pain, and now it was Fat Mama holding him in the awful hammerlock, and it was Frieda's mouth pressing against his in a kiss that bruised his lips against his teeth. He twisted his head but couldn't avoid her hungry mouth, her tongue slipping through his tight lips, and he heard a chattering of automatic rifles and choruses of screams.

She was moaning and mumbling, "Come. Come, my sweet Aquarius," and he felt her urgent thighs and her hand teasing him into her slippery warmth, and wet velvet sliding around him, and her excited breathing in gasps just like his own, and he couldn't bear it any longer, he felt his thighs thrusting up against hers, his tongue inside her mouth, their lips gliding, and he burst in a terrible throbbing of pain and joy and wonder, and he was a virgin no more, no more, and he lay there under her steady swaying, feeling his penis gradually soften, and her rhythm slow, and she whispered, "I am to teach you how to love," and he wept in the sharpest guilt of his adolescent life, as Fat Mama released his arm and Frieda slid off him at last and stood up like a winning wrestler, and she was Jessie again, wearing her father's faded jersey and pulling on her panties like a jock.

"Now, smart-ass," she sneered, "you're no better than the rest of us."

The light had gone out of the dingy world, and all he could see, stirring gently in the gloom, was the hanging body of his father. Frieda's hollow voice echoed through a cave: "The truth is for the second set of books."

TWENTY

THE SOUND of moans echoed in his ears. Where was he? He tried to turn over, but he was caught in a straitjacket of twisted sheets, his right arm bent behind him. He yanked himself out of the tangle and lay there on the mattress, in the cool of sweat and semen, panting.

Motel. He was in a motel. Steak and Lobster. Julian was still pacing heavily in the adjoining room. Why? What time was it?

Getting light outside.

The wet nightmare stayed in his mind. He closed his eyes. He hated the past, every contact with the world an error, a personal foul. Nancy: he tried to think of Nancy's face, her hair, her breasts. But he was swinging blind. Strike three.

He couldn't sleep again, scared to now. So he was awake when Julian burst through the door, shaking the floor like an earthquake and heralding the dawn.

"Listen to this again. It's all beginning to make sense." He was carrying a huge black book and squinting at his crumpled handwritten notes.

" 'And over the central cave burned the hunter by winter nights, the bear by summer. And at dawn on Midsummer Day the rays of the fiery lion fall *directly through the twin stones* and kindle the flames at the portals of the holy place, lighting for that one moment the sacred way to the mystery, to the central cave, to the holy altar, to the treasures, a guide eternal to the faithful, that the central cave be never lost again.' "

Julian huffed. In his eagerness he had read it all in one breath.

"Now. You ready? Look!" He pulled the curtains. The sun was a perfect disc between the two steep crags in the east. The Steak and Lobster Inn lay directly in the path of murky sunlight.

"And what day is it, Frank?"

"June, let's see, twenty-fifth?"

"The day after Midsummer Day, right?" Julian was triumphant. "So we've found something at last, after all the false starts. We've found 'the portals of the holy place,' the 'sacred way to the mystery, to the central cave.' "

But Frank's mind, foggy with the lingering nightmare, stuck at this. The day after her birthday, air and water. He growled. "Midsummer Day? But the calendar shifts, doesn't it? The sun shifts, the solstice? Midsummer Day should be the twenty-second, now. And besides . . ." He looked out the window at the two crags in the east. "You call those 'twin stones'? They're hills, for God's sake. 'Stones' means—like Stonehenge."

"Don't be so literal, that's been our whole trouble. We're translating a pretty strange document, after all, Latin transliterated into runes by scribes whose stock-in-trade was metaphor. The more technical and literal we get, the less likely we are to see what they meant. The truth may never play you false," he added sonorously, waving an index finger, "but she can be a tricky mistress, all the same."

Julian was pacing again. He pulled a Baby Ruth bar out of his pocket and went on. "And anyway, everything out here is rock, limestone. The hills *are* 'stones,' you see? And midsummer is midsummer, regardless of what calendar you're using. It'll take more than a few measly centuries to shift that fiery lion out of its position between those hills."

"So?"

"So we've just discovered something. That cave under the church is no more the central cave than a fruit cellar. It's in the wrong place. Look."

Frank looked out. The two church spires were still dark, in the morning shadows of the twin hills.

Julian stopped by Frank's pillow and gazed down earnestly, eyes gleaming, belly atremble with discovery. "The entrance to the real central cave has got to be in the path of the sun. Which means it could be here, right here, under our feet."

Frank was still trying to get the nightmare out of his mind. He struggled with this new thought. "In a *motel*?"

"The whole county is a honeycomb of caverns, tunnels, sinkholes, grottoes, pits. Karst country, the limestone does it, the underground rivers." Julian popped the last bite of candy in his mouth without interrupting himself. "It's a natural for Vikings. Think of all those caves of theirs, the trolls, the cavern burials, Loki and his serpent, legendary chests of jewels always hidden deep in the earth. No wonder the Vikings found a home here."

He fumbled in his pockets, but the candy bars were gone. He sighed. "The point is, that's not the half of it. The point is, there's something here that goes way beyond Loki and Freyr and Wodan. Vikings weren't the only ones enamored of caves. And karst goes everywhere, binds the world together. Limestone, Frank, born in the ooze at the bottom of ancient seas, it puts a girdle round the world, from Kashmir to Sweden, from Persia to Indiana. Karst is the mothering earth of caves, the home of mankind for untold centuries, much longer than we've dared to live up here on the surface. Frank, what's the sign of the summer solstice?"

Another of Julian's sudden switches. Frank was surprised enough to sit up in bed. "The zodiac sign?" Frieda's rejection came back to him, a twist of the knife, and he knew at once: he loved her more than ever. But he put that aside, resolutely, and thought a moment. "It must be Cancer, isn't it?"

"To us it's Cancer. To the whole Graeco-Roman world it's been Cancer." Julian smacked the scholarly tome he was carrying, like a parson thumping holy writ. "But two thousand years before the Roman empire it wasn't Cancer, it was Leo, as it ought to be, the kingly sun itself, fiery energy, conquering force. Given millennia enough, the sun does shift, after all, has to, the precession of the equinoxes does it. Makes a total hash of astrology, of course. But in the ancient Eastern zodiacs, the sign of the summer solstice was always the fiery lion, the unconquered sun."

A jigsaw sky was fitting together. Frank felt like a savage at an eclipse.

" 'At dawn on Midsummer Day the rays of the fiery lion fall through the twin stones.' That's not Viking talk, it's Persian. Chaldean."

Frank got up and pulled on his pants, feeling giddy.

"Look out here." Julian took him into the adjoining room and pointed to the swinging brown shingle showing the steer and the lobster. "How old would you say that sign was?"

"How would I know? Can't be very old, it's wood."

"In Norway there are wooden temples that have been standing for a thousand years." Julian pulled a sheet of motel stationery out of a drawer, folded it over, and slapped it on his writing desk. "Draw a scorpion, on the right, there."

Grudgingly, feeling more and more trapped, Frank drew a crude scorpion.

"Not bad." Julian held it at arm's length like a connoisseur. "Now draw a bull to the left of it. Like the one you killed at the fair."

Frank's memory was vivid. He drew again.

"Fine." Julian was beaming. "Do you see what it is? Do you know what it means?"

Frank indulged him. "No, Uncle Julian, what does it mean?"

"Iconography. The bull and the scorpion. You've just drawn two of the central icons of Mithra, god of the sun, *soli invicto Mithrae*." He laughed, a gurgle of triumph. "Now look at the letterhead."

Frank unfolded the paper. At the top of the page, the words "The Steak and Lobster Inn" made a rainbow semicircle above the printed figures.

Frank's skin prickled, like a swimmer come out of salt water. Julian went on laughing, his beady eyes bright with victory. "The holy place," he gloated. "We're *in* the holy place."

TWENTY-ONE

JULIAN couldn't calm down. "It's got to be here. I know I'd be clapped in the loony bin for saying it in public, but we're plop in the bull's-eye of a cosmic target, and right outside that window are the corrupted icons of Mithra. So there's no question about it, is there? We're sitting here on top of a Mithreum! The central cave. And now, by God, we're going to find it. We start by getting every coin you can find. For the candy machine. I spent all my own change last night, and we'll have to skip breakfast.

Frank's eyes opened wide for the first time that morning.

"Can't be helped. A pity, but our gracious hostess took pains to hornswoggle us before, and—it hurts to say it—she can't be trusted. Nor her Aquarius-stricken daughter, I'm afraid. The truth is, we don't know who we can trust now."

Frank gathered up pain in his chest, embraced it. He remembered his first sight of her, that lovely angry face, the arms away from her sides, palms out, all innocence, her fingers caressing things: profit and loss, profit and loss. Without warning, he felt the tears again.

"So we'll have to slip past them and find the basement of this place without being seen. But there's one more thing." He pointed out the window again. Beyond the silver of his Stingray, Frank saw an orange Firebird, with the usual bumper sticker.

I WILL GIVE UP MY GUN WHEN THEY PRY IT
OUT OF MY COLD, DEAD FINGERS

The Firebird was riddled with bullet holes, the rear window gun racks empty.

"I mean down there. And over there. See?"

Frank looked again, and caught his breath. At the far right and far left, sheriff's squad cars were parked. No one was in them.

"I don't know who drove them in here, Olaf's men or Magnus's, but somebody's snooping around, and sure as hell they're laying for us. This movie's in its last reel."

Panicky, Frank grabbed loose change from a drawer, peeked right and left out the door, and led the way. It was burglar work, tiptoeing down the hall toward the main building, working the candy machine, sneaking past the glass door beyond which Fat Mama and Frieda were serving early breakfasts, ducking out of sight when the two women, carrying trays, turned their way, then slipping into the motel office, probing doorways, dead-ending into closets, and finally finding what they were looking for, the stairway to the basement. Julian flicked the switch, and a bare bulb glowed in the distance.

Not exactly a basement, as it turned out. Halfway down, the wooden stairway ended, and they were descending steps cut in stone. The basement was a natural basin of earth.

"A sinkhole. Perfect! And over there's the entrance."

Julian's hunches were paying off. At one side of the sinkhole there was an opening in the ground as big as the doorway they had just come through. They crossed over to it, and Julian looked around. "Chances are, they'd have a supply of candles here somewhere."

Right again. There were candles and matches in a metal box near the hole. Julian took a pocketful, lit a candle for each of them, and without hesitating, stepped into the hole. "Down we go," he called back.

Julian's hunches, Julian's hypotheses, Julian's truth: Frank couldn't resist following. He moved into the cool darkness, the candle flickering in the steady breeze that blew against his face. The gray stone walls were undulant with erosion and sometimes barely wide enough for Julian to wiggle through. The passage twisted occasionally, dipped and descended, went on and on. In the distance there was the sound of rushing water.

"Look here." Julian stopped abruptly. Off to the right there had once been a connecting corridor, but now it was blocked off, full of limestone rubble.

"Breakdown. Earthquakes cause it. Limestone's very brittle."

Frank thought he felt a tremor. "Julian, what was that?"

Julian looked away. "What?"

"That—like an earthquake."

Julian wouldn't look at him. "You ever been through an earthquake?"

"No."

"Then how do you know? Besides, I didn't notice anything. Nothing at all. Look here."

He pointed to the wall. There was a round hole at shoulder height, about two inches in diameter.

"Now look up there."

He held up his candle. The top of the corridor, a foot or two above their heads, was black.

"Torch socket. Must be all along the passage, we've been missing them. Come on."

"What about that tremor?"

"Imagination." Julian lumbered off, his candle playing shadows down the corridor.

Frank wondered if Julian was lying about not feeling the quake. He looked behind and thought he saw a glimmer of light. Was it real? Anyway, he couldn't go back now, not with Julian plunging ahead, and with the answers to all their questions finally—maybe—so close. He followed the leading candle and the ghostly sound of Julian's voice.

"The Edda says Thor was the grandson of Priam, Viking gods spawned in the topless towers of Ilium, imagine that. Odin, wandering from Troy to Sweden, to set up shop, Asians in Scandinavia, holding on there, pagan gods, till Olaf the Holy drove them out to Iceland." Frank heard him laughing. "Nonsense, of course, pure myth. The real connection had to be later, much later, fifteen, sixteen centuries after Troy burned."

How far had they come, down this rocky, wavering passage? Frank looked back again, candle held high, half expecting to see pursuers, but there were only flickering shadows.

Occasionally Julian would point to things—another torch socket, another blocked passage. The sound of rushing water kept getting louder. Julian was walking faster and faster, squeezing through the tight places, a stiff clip for a fat man, even downhill.

"Frieda's little story is closer to it. The black bull, Armin—read Ahriman, evil king of darkness—and the scorpions, too, that all fits in, the friar, Freyr in the central cave with his sword and his torch, his slash at the bull's heart, that all makes sense now."

He stopped abruptly. The passage had ceased to be a passage. The walls had widened out, and ahead of them was an opening, a cavern so big, so full of blackness, that their candles showed only the vague ghosts of things: dim fairylands of white stalactites, helictites blown by cavern winds into the image of gnarled trees, stone flowers sprouting from the walls like coral forests in the sea, rimstone brimming over the edges of frozen pools. Frank stared. The beauty of it was terrifying.

The sound of rushing water had become a roar, an invisible waterfall.

Julian bent forward, examining the path at their feet. Just ahead of them it disappeared, dropped off to nothing. He picked up a stone and tossed it over the edge. For seconds there was no sound, then finally a splash.

Frank tried not to look down.

Julian was still searching the path and the walls, talking absently. "The deep caves, places of dread—the perpetual dark, the danger of getting lost, lost forever, the fear of flash floods, rats, rabid bats—and yet our most ancient hope, the magic bulls at Lascaux, the holy stalagmite in Nepal, lingam of Shiva, the mysterious goat horns deep in Uzbekistan."

Frank couldn't stop staring at the fantastic crystalline beauty, delicate, massive, ominous. He strained his eyes into the rushing darkness.

"Here it is," Julian called. "Come this way." On a narrow ledge they crept along, following a series of marks cut in the cavern wall, hugging the stone and deliberating every small step. The wall marks had the appearance of runes, the scribbles of Wong's parchments, of Frieda's bracelets.

They inched on for several minutes, Julian talking all the time. "This isn't *the* cave, you know. Can't be. Too big, for one thing. Mithraic caves have certain characteristics, layouts. But I'll bet we're getting close."

The clamor of the waterfall increased. Frank felt a fine mist on his face. As the cryptic marks continued, the footing got more precarious on the slippery ledge. Finally he understood: the path led directly under the waterfall. He froze, fingernails clawing the smooth stone wall.

"We can't make it. We'll slip off of here." It was like talking in a barrel.

"Listen, if they could carve those runes, we can follow them. Stay close to the wall."

They crept ahead. The waterfall was spraying out over the ledge, enveloping them, the mist making little rainbows around the worried candle flames.

Then Julian's candle disappeared. Frank called out, but there was no answer. He sucked in his breath and held it. No scream, no splash, no terrible thudding of flesh, only the rushing water. He edged forward a few inches, then a little more, his legs tense. The wall made a sharp angle to the left, the ledge became a corridor: another angle, to the right, then two more turns, a zigzag. The sound of the waterfall was muted, almost silenced by the baffles of limestone. At last he saw the other candle again, ahead of him in a new cave, and his whole body went limp with relief. Farther ahead, in the gloomy distance, was an incredible thing—a flaming lamp.

Julian was standing there peering at the walls. "This is the one, Frank! Look, it's perfect, nature improved upon, the walls hacked away for a twelve-sided room, one side for each sign of the zodiac, and a doorway in every side, the cave as cosmos, winds and seasons and planets, all dedicated to Mithra—father, maker, and mediator."

Frank's common sense rebelled at this.

"It's the whole world, the universe, bending down to that altar." Julian pulled out a Mounds bar and munched on it.

Through a double row of stone benches they walked slowly toward the altar. The feeble oil lamp was burning beside a bas-relief altar-piece set in the face of the rock. Carved on its surface were more runes and the two familiar symbols, a bull and scorpion so vivid that they seemed to leap out of some ancient nightmare.

The cold crept along Frank's skin. Hidden eyes, malignant slits, were peering at him from the twelve doorways. Who tended a lamp down here? He squinted into the black recesses of the cave. Shadows quivered there like furtive spirits.

"The Steak and Lobster!" Julian laughed. "Frank, on the great stele of Nebuchadnezzar, emperor of Babylon, heir to the Chaldeans, are carved the bull and scorpion, the spring and autumn of our lives. Back even as far as Hammurabi, back to the dawn of the epic gods, the bull and the scorpion have always been birth and death, spring and fall, rise and set, the equinoxes of our coming and going."

"The Steak and Lobster," Frank murmured, incredulous.

Julian sat down on the stone bench, laughing, or sobbing. "Think of the distance he's come. Born of a virgin somewhere in Asia, sung in the oldest Vedas, 'Mithra sustaineth both earth and heaven,' passing in the fullness of time to Persia, god of light to Darius and Xerxes, the unconquered sun, then marching to Rome with the pious legions, lord of the bull and scorpion, carried to the imperial frontier, to the Rhine and the Danube and the *Limes*, long wall of superstitious fear, studded all its length with karst caverns, traded to Vikings with Roman gold and bright barbaric stones, then banished from his northern fastnesses by the Christian fanatic kings, Knut the Great, Olaf the Holy, driven across the terrible western sea, and come to rest in the caves of Indiana, sun-god in a land of smog . . ."

Julian trailed off. Frank felt the bathos of his triumph, and pitied him. He could amost have sworn the earth was shaking again.

TWENTY-TWO

THE OIL LAMP was too dim to help much. Julian was fussing at the altarpiece on the cave wall, holding his candle this way, then that.

"What do the runes say?"

"What they're supposed to say, '*soli invicto Mithrae*.' What I don't find is any sign of a hoard." He poked around for a while, then sat down again and tore the wrapper off a Powerhouse. Except for the muffled waterfall, the cave was quiet. Disturbingly quiet.

"They know, though," Julian finally muttered. "Sybil knows, all right. That's why they've kept us out of here, never mentioned the place to us at all. Couple of city slickers down for the fair, why should we be trusted?"

Julian, in his hour of triumph, was sulking.

"No, they're not like that. Not Frieda, anyway. She wouldn't play tricks on us."

Julian snorted. "What about all that astrology nonsense last night? That was pretty tricky."

Frieda's rejection swept over him again, tumbling him into the murky depths of his nightmare. He fought it off with silent incanta-tions: *I love her, I love her.*

"No, she means it. I know it's silly, but she really believes it, she isn't faking."

"Well, more's the pity. Anyway, they're obviously flimflamming us." Julian moved to the altarpiece again, irritated. "Where the hell's the gold?"

"Sure it's crazy, that hocus-pocus, but we're all a little crazy, aren't we? Anyway, I love her." It was out of his hands.

"So be it," Julian grumbled, preoccupied. "I'm beginning to think we're not at the end of all this yet. Something's still missing. Like a jigsaw puzzle with one side ragged."

I love her, I love her.

"If she'd only talk to me, we could make it up. I think. I mean, you can't love somebody one minute and break it off the next, I know that now. Even if you wanted to, it's just not possible."

"Yes, that's true." The grave voice spoke from shadows, scaring Frank. Julian whirled like a trapped thief.

"How did *you* get here?"

"The same way you did. I come here all the time." She glided soundlessly, a little off balance, to Frank's side, the loveliest girl in the world. The nightmare came back in a rush, but when she touched his hand, it vanished. "You're right," she said, "it's not possible to stop. I love you."

Frank's candle was making rainbows. He reached for her.

She pulled away. "Wait, I have to apologize first. Explain, I mean. No, I mean apologize." Words spilled out in a rush, breathless. "You see, I was so crazy and furious and scared last night—Kent, Sigrid, all that shooting, I couldn't take it at all. Something in me just stran-gled on the rage and the fear, and it left me helpless, and . . ."

As she talked and remembered, tears glistened in the lamplight. "I guess I was out of my mind a little."

Profit and loss: she put her arms around Frank's waist and spoke into his shirt. "Mama gave me a sleeping pill and put me to bed. But later I woke up, and I wasn't scared any more, I was mad, I mean really furious at those murderers and their guns, always their cowardly guns. And I was ashamed, too, of what I'd said to you, and I wanted to come to you then, in the night."

"I wish you had."

"But I had to do something first. I couldn't just lie there any more, stiff and sweating with rage. So I got my tools and went back to the park."

"My God, Frieda, that's dangerous."

"Two nights running, yes. And it began to rain." Her voice rose, feverish. "But I kept on going. I had to get one for Sigrid, and for Kent. And I did, two big bulldozers. I beat hell out of them, there in the rain, mashed the bastards good, pulled their guts out, totalled them!"

She got a grip on herself and looked at him strangely, that sly, ambiguous glance. "Later, when I was on my way home through the alleys, a night bird sang, and I looked around, and the rain had stopped and the clouds had broken up, and I could see stars. And all of a sudden I heard myself yelling at them, *liars, liars, liars, liars!* There in the dark alley, all alone, I was screaming at the stars. And then I missed you so much, and I wanted to tell you, that the stars do lie, and you really are an Aquarius. And I really do love you."

"But Julian says I'm a Pisces."

"That's just calendar talk. It doesn't matter."

Hope and fear went caroming around his chest. Frank toyed with salvation, fingered loss, tried first for the easy victory. "You mean you don't believe it any more—about the sun, and the planets, and destiny?"

She hesitated, fidgeted a little, and looked down. "I'm not sure what I believe now. But one thing I do know, and must have known always. If something is destroying love, then it's—well, it's wrong, that's all."

It wasn't easy for her, obviously, this melting away of a lifetime of faith. Her voice wavered, faded, came back strong. "I loved you for the wrong reasons before. Delusions, superstition. But now I know, you are an Aquarius, no matter when you were born, regardless of the phony stars and horoscopes. Because you're truly generous, I know that. You're truly noble and understanding and gentle and, well, all the things an Aquarius is. So when I saw you tiptoeing past, in the hallway, I followed you, to tell you, to apologize."

"Frieda, I hate to say this, but . . ." His voice had more edge to it than he had planned. It wasn't obeying him well now: the moment of truth. He took a deep breath. "Those admirable qualities don't really fit me. Not at all."

Julian's voice echoed from the far side of the cave. "Don't be a fool, Frank."

But it had to be said, had to be risked, or the old faults would always be down there, ready to shift and destroy. Frank relished the self-indulgence of rectitude, a far, far better thing . . . "Frieda, the truth is, I'm not a bit generous. I'm greedy. And I'm not noble, I'm a crook."

She couldn't grasp it that quickly. Her eyes squinted in bewilderment.

"Julian and I, we're a pair of swindlers. We ghostwrite illegal dissertations for a living."

"Not illegal, son, no."

"Maybe not exactly illegal. But immoral. Unscrupulous. They ask for fact and we feed them fiction, for a price, a high price."

He watched her bewilderment grow, felt the pain of her pain reach every nerve in his body. But he could tell she still didn't really believe it, and he had to deliver the final, ugly blow. "Frieda, do you understand truth and falsehood now, after all you've been through? Well, how about this? 'Coordinated multiple-range testing procedures indicate successful concept transfers in 83.7 percent of all cases of subsystem stimuli giving responses above the seventieth percentile . . .' "

"Stop it." She was grim now.

He spoke gently. "You see? My father always said, they've caught you when you catch yourself. Your noble Aquarius is nothing but a con man."

"You know that isn't true."

Proud in his self-flagellation, Frank wasn't prepared for flat denial. "What?"

"I know it isn't true. I mean you may have written those things, but that's not what I know about you. I'm telling you I know you.

This isn't superstition any more. You're as honest as the daylight. Even if you did those things, it wasn't really you, but some perversion of you, some temporary . . ."

"My father always said, show me how you spend your days, and I'll tell you how you spend your nights." Frank paused, confused. Had his father really said that, or had he made it up himself? He couldn't remember.

"Your father must have been some kind of idiot."

Frank was incensed, then, in a freshening moment, liberated. He smiled. She instantly softened.

"I'm sorry. I guess I shouldn't have said that."

"It's all right." Carefully, like a sick man trying to walk, he put one word after another. "I think I've always wanted to say that myself."

Horizons were stretching out in his forehead, rolling green under clear blue skies. It occurred to him like a new, a highly original thought: he loved his father.

"What I mean is, lots of people get off to a bad start, fall into bad habits, without really thinking. We all make mistakes. But you understand now."

She kissed him, and the world washed clean all over.

To be good . . .

"Well spoken." Things had obviously worked out to Julian's satisfaction; he was all business. "But what was that you were saying before? You come here all the time?"

"We tend the eternal flame, Mama and I, it's our job. And in the winter, when it's cold outside and it feels so cozy here, I come down a lot. I even bring a sleeping bag sometimes and camp overnight."

"In the winter? You stay down here, in the winter?"

"Sometimes. Mama worries about me, but I tell her when spring comes, I'll be up there all the time."

"Damnedest mishmash I ever heard!" Julian erupted. "So you go back in the spring, do you? To your mother?"

His outburst made her defensive. "I suppose it sounds silly to you, but I feel I belong here when it gets so cold, so dead outside. Just listen for a minute."

The soft rush of water outside the sacred cave, the quiet inside.

When she finally spoke, her voice was hushed. "Mama used to bring me here and tell me what her mother told her, about when all the world was like this, everywhere—quiet, and the music of clear water, and the air so clean, and everything fresh. And we used to close our eyes and try to hear birds singing, and see puffy white clouds in a jewel of a sky, and shimmering trees, and bright flowers in rolling meadows."

"Yes," Frank breathed. "And now . . ."

"Oh, now." She smiled so sadly Frank wanted to weep. "Now, in a cave is the only place where you can feel pure. You have to be deep in the earth now to feel the world wants you in it at all."

She pulled a daisy out of her belt. "Here. For you." She tucked it in his buttonhole. "Keep it, and if you're ever tempted to write one of those—things, again, if the money tempts you again, then look at this and remember, that spring is always here, in the mind, and love—we're all love has." She had backed away, and stood by the altar. "You understand now, how to be spring yourself."

And he did understand, that was the awesome thing. He knew, as if he'd always known, the last melting of snow, the smell of freshly turned earth, the tiny green leaves.

"You make that all sound more like mythology than spelunking," Julian said.

Softly: "I guess that's how I feel it." She didn't know Julian well enough to have detected the subtle sarcasm in his voice.

But Frank did.

And so did Fat Mama, who stepped barefoot out of the shadows, stately in her flowing white robes.

TWENTY-THREE

ON'T MOCK HER, Capricorn. She's telling the truth. And she knows nothing about the black stone."

"The black stone!" Julian echoed. He sat down on the bench abruptly, as if pushed. "Sybil, really!"

"You said there was a piece of the puzzle missing, didn't you?"

So she had been listening, too.

The lamp flickered. Fat Mama seemed mysterious, threatening. "Think it through. What piece was it likely to be, once you got the unconquered sun?"

"The black stone. Impossible!" Julian's voice was a complaint. "Mother of all . . ." He choked.

Fat Mama prompted him. "That's right, mother of all, mistress of man . . ."

Julian joined in, his voice unsteady. "Mistress of man and of the beasts of the field, spirit of plains and woods and mountains, blessing of grain in every land, the fruitful friendly earth itself."

He stood up, ripping open a Payday bar, obviously trying to come to grips with some new speculation. "So that's why you wouldn't show us this cave."

Fat Mama folded her arms, mysterious as night. "I told you to stay out of the church, didn't I? How much help do you need? And you know it has to be a quest, not a simple gift. But I followed you anyway, to be sure you got it right this time."

Frank held on to Frieda's hand, feeling stupid again. "Would you two mind letting me in on your secrets? What stone are you talking about?"

Julian's voice was noticeably more tenor than usual, and jerky. "Meteorite, probably. At Troy, of all places. Birthplace of Thor and Odin, the Edda says." He seemed to consider it for a moment, then shook it off. "Alien stuff, anyway, the black stone, not of this earth, inexplicable back then, therefore sacred. Powerful. The Romans wanted it for defense purposes, what with Hannibal still roaming the countryside, burning and pillaging."

Fat Mama picked up the story. "And they got it, the black stone, mother of the gods, Magna Mater, carried from Asia Minor to Rome, and greeted there with a spectacular holiday, senators, matrons, legionaries, slaves, vestals, all of them out there cheering, doing homage to the final act in the Trojan emigration . . ."

Julian interrupted. "Rome in the embrace of the Orient, *ab oriente ad occidentum!*"

Pitying Julian, unstrung by this cultural outrage, Frank protested. "All right, all right, but how could it be here?"

"Use your imagination today, Pisces. If Mithra, why not the Magna Mater?"

"Yes, why not?" Julian's voice was an octave above normal now. He was laughing sporadically. "Syncretism!" he half-shouted. "With syncretism in full blast, Cybele, mother of the gods, comes to embrace all the other nature goddesses, and by then she's also consort to Mithra, both of them worshiped in sanctuaries under the earth, both of them sacred in the blood of bulls. Why yes, of course, if the one, why not the other?"

He looked around the cave, and when he spoke again, his voice was under control, a murmur. "Inevitable, you might say, human nature being what it is, the awful mysteries of Mithra complemented by the maternal presence, Cybele a humanizing warmth in that dark Mithraic sacrifice—love, the other face of fear."

I am to teach you how to love. Frieda squeezed Frank's hand, and he recognized the awesome implications twisting a mesh around him: *Do you ever think of yourself as God?* He felt fraudulent, a miscast actor.

Julian was pacing about clumsily now, and Frank could have sworn there were tears in his eyes. He stopped and pointed at Fat Mama. "Yes, if the one, why not the other? The truth, Sybil."

Fat Mama glanced at him briefly, then walked to the altarpiece and touched it. It swung forward slowly, like the door of a wall safe. Frank gasped. In the spacious cavity behind the altarpiece was a large black stone, and heaped around the stone, a great jumble of gold and silver: gold bridle-mounts and silver stirrups, heaps of coins, tawny disc-brooches patterned with gold filigree and fantastic beasts, intricately figured gold pendants, neck rings of braided gold, and solid gold arm rings in the shape of serpents. Fat Mama took Frieda's bracelets and her own locket and laid them beside the others. Colors and shapes blended.

In the shadows, Julian's moist eyes glowed like a leopard's.

"There," she said, "that's the whole thing. Does it help to clear your mind? I've ministered to it ever since my mother died. Frieda will tend it after I'm gone, mind the eternal flame."

"Never!"

In the shifting lamplight, the rough voice was connected only to the glint of a rifle in one of the twelve doorways. "Get over there against the wall. Make it fast!"

Olaf moved in as Fat Mama, speechless, backed away from the altar. The gun barrel was shaking. In a moment all four of them were against the cave wall, Julian puffing indignantly. Trickles of sweat itched along Frank's skin. Frieda took Frank's hand and gazed at him; her hand was cool and steady.

"Years," Olaf panted. "You had me buffaloed, Sybil. Took me years to find this place. But by God, it was worth it. Magnus can have his tin badge now, it's not worth a damn without the gold, or the hope of it. And me . . ." Olaf cackled. "Pretty soon I'll be in Canada, with all this loot." He rested the gun on the altar and began stuffing coins, bracelets, and brooches into a large canvas bag.

Fat Mama's rich voice echoed off the twelve walls. "You can't do this, Olaf, it's sacrilege!"

Frank marveled. Here in the cave, regal in her white robes, she made pleading sound godlike.

Olaf fondled a golden bowl. "All the time I put in, heisting those parchments from the cornerstone of the old church, sweating out those idiot translations . . ."

"Wong!" Julian burped sharply. "You're J. Randolph Wong! And you're not one damn bit Chinese!"

"I *was* J. Randolph Wong, among other names. Now I'm a millionaire, on my way to the pleasure capitals of the world."

Frank had a quick vision of the aged Olaf, wafted on a litter from casino to casino, bordello to bordello.

"But I've been hunting for you, Wong. I've got to ask you some questions!" Julian sounded desperate. "Listen to me, this is important! About those parchments—where are they?"

Olaf grabbed his rifle and spattered steel into the rock just over Julian's head. Frank pulled Frieda's face into his chest, trying to ward off the ricocheting splinters of limestone.

"Parchments! You fat-ass egghead, you want to know about parchments, do you? Sheet after sheet of them you translate, week after week, and for what? To change runes into that horseshit jargon. What good did that do me? Were you after the gold yourself, you phony? Was that your game?"

Julian sputtered, and in the dim light Frank could have sworn he was blushing.

Olaf breathed hard, calming down. "I thought so. Well, in the end I had to tail you, day and night, and find it for myself. And I did it, by God, I've won. You want to know about the parchments, buddy? I burned them."

He threw more gold into the bag. Julian sagged back against the stone wall, head in hands, moaning.

Fat Mama, pale after the gunfire, was somber. "If only you were a reverent man."

Olaf snickered. "Then I'd be down on my knees to you, like the rest of these hicks, right? Not a chance. I may have lost the election, but I'm going to have the last laugh."

Olaf had scooped out as much gold as the bag and his pockets would hold, and now looked with regret at the rest. "Well, we've come to the happy ending, haven't we? The part where we rub out the witnesses. Have you said your prayers, fat lady?" The rifle barrel eased up and pointed at the four victims. Frieda hugged Frank, and he loved life in that moment more than anyone ever had, anywhere, because he loved Frieda, loved her, loved her.

There was a moment of total immobility in the cave, and then rifle fire splintered the silence. Frieda held him tight, and Frank clung to her steadiness for one last moment.

But it was Olaf slumping onto the altar and springing leaks all over his body. His rifle clattered on rock, and then the bag of treasure slipped from his fingers.

Before the nasal voice echoed through the cave, Frank knew it had to be Magnus.

"I could have taken him, dead or alive, any time in the last twelve hours," Magnus crowed, "but it wasn't good enough. This is how I wanted it. A time to be born, and a time to die. Scorpio, Scorpio!" He raised his eyes to the altar. "O divine mediator, let the bull of our springtime coming and the scorpion of our autumn going tell our souls' salvation."

He picked up the bag of golden treasure. "So this is where you've held out on us all these years, Sybil. Well, well, well, what a pleasant surprise." He fingered the gold. "And what a pity I can't permit you to share this pleasure with me." He straightened up and raised the automatic rifle.

"You mustn't, father! It's a violation."

Magnus squeezed off a burst that missed her narrowly, spraying all four of them with broken limestone. Frank covered Frieda's body with his own and felt the shards nicking his cheeks. Blood trickled warm through the phony beard. He felt the whole scene repeating, repeating. He wanted desperately to do something, to save them from this cavern burial, but he was rigid with fear.

Magnus's rifle toyed with them, pointing at one, then another, spewing short bursts of bullets around them, cat and mouse.

"A holy sacrifice," Magnus laughed. "The supreme sacrifice, truly acceptable unto the Lord."

"Stop it, father!" Fat Mama's voice was sharp now, but she stood motionless, one arm raised like a statue, mother and protectress, passionate and tender.

Desperation was crowding out Frank's fear. He considered trying to charge the rifle. Hopeless. He'd be blown away before he moved two steps. Julian stood beside Fat Mama, unable to get a word out, his arms sawing the air like a politician's. In the shadow of the two bulky people, Frieda stooped down and then slipped something into Frank's hand—hard, rough—a chunk of limestone, the size of a baseball. "Understand," she whispered.

The touch of that small rough hand freed Frank from paralysis. He felt the rock snug in his pitching hand, and felt the roar go through his spine as Magnus squeezed off a burst close to Julian's head, playing with his blubbery fear, relishing it, and Frank saw the love in Frieda's darkened eyes and felt the earth shake as he threw the beanball and saw Magnus's forehead split red and heard the rifle smashing steel into the overhead stone and felt the earth shake again as the huge slab fell, burying the priest of a thousand years of order.

"Earthquake!" Big Mama yelled. "Haul ass out of here before the big ones hit!"

No one needed urging. Their hands made a chain, with Frieda leading the way out of the cave, under the waterfall, along the sheer wall. And even after her candle blew out in the rushing winds, she pressed on unerringly, up and up through the twisting passages, Julian and Fat Mama laboring on behind her, panting through the dark like great tired animals.

If only, if only—it was a throbbing in Frank's mind, a pain in every pulse—*if only we can beat the big shocks*. His legs were going rubber, partly fatigue, partly fear.

Someone tripped. The sudden wrench at his arm spun him half around, and he heard a big body thud into rock, and another one fall into it with a huff.

Julian was groaning. "My knees! Oh, God, they're broken!"

Fat Mama was moaning incoherently. Frieda was scratching

matches, lighting a candle. Julian's groans continued, painful to hear.

If only, if only. . .

In the small flicker of Frieda's candle, the two tumbled forms seemed enormously complicated. Working frantically, in a clumsy dream, Frank tried to get them sorted out, arms and legs separated, great hulks pulled to a sitting position.

"Come on, Julian, we've got to hurry. Here, put an arm over my shoulder, that's it. Now, *now!*"

Julian made it halfway, then fell back, rocking and groaning.

Frieda had been coaxing Fat Mama up a little, to hands and knees, then a little more—one leg, the other—and finally she was up, wobbly but ready to go.

"Come on, Sybil's up, you've got to try harder."

"I am trying. But I must have come down on something sharp, the knees won't work. You'll have to go on without me."

"Don't be silly, for God's sake. Try!" Claustrophobia was panicking him. Frank got a shoulder under one of Julian's arms and tugged. No good. He began to despair.

"Let me help." Frieda got under the other arm. "Ready? OK, one, two, three!" Julian came up halfway and faltered again, the massive inertia staggering Frank. He gasped and pulled.

"Heave, damn it!" Frieda yelled, her voice a convulsive wheezing. Fat Mama pushed from behind, and they all put their backs into it. Frank could feel his eyes bulging with the strain.

Finally, unbelievably, Julian was upright.

"Now move!" And Frieda was off again, holding Fat Mama's hand, her candle a tiny guide ahead of them, Frank shoring up his creaking, groaning, cursing uncle, moving along precariously, but moving.

At last they were at the entrance, then out into the sinkhole, under the bare light bulb, and Julian's legs had made it almost to the wooden stairs when the big quakes came, sifting the rock like gravel. They heard fierce grinding sounds, the caving-in of subterranean passages. Knocked sprawling again, they looked back. The cave entrance was blocked with rubble.

It took them painful minutes to recover, to get up and work their way to the stairs.

"Five hundred feet," Julian groaned. "The limestone is five hundred feet thick around here. Magnus and Olaf have found themselves the deepest, hardest tomb in history."

He paused, troubled. Fat Mama, crawling up to daylight, was sobbing a loss of her own.

"And so has the black stone," Julian added, his voice cracking. "And all that beautiful, beautiful gold."

TWENTY-FOUR

THEY WERE SAFE, all together around the table, at breakfast in the afternoon, Frieda sitting close to Frank, Fat Mama gently massaging Julian's tender knees while he ate.

Even with Olaf and Magnus buried, Frank couldn't seem to relax. The feeling of something pursuing him wouldn't go away. He picked at his food.

Julian was munching the magic sausages. "I still don't see how a Viking settlement could have been here all this time without being discovered."

"Why, by mingling, by blending into the wallpaper." Fat Mama grinned at Julian. Whatever she had lost down there in the cave, her resilience had survived. She sat up and sipped her coffee. Julian leaned over and took his turn massaging her knees. She grunted with pleasure. They were as domestic as an old married couple.

She spoke again, gazing into her cup. "To be alive means having to change, after all, and we've lived on this spot for ages, our people have, since the days of the Mound Builders. It's all in our legends, our old tales. Ages ago we got along OK with the Choctaws, the

Delawares, and later the Shawnees. We were tougher than any of them, and better armed, with bronze and iron. We came to respect each other, smoked the pipe together in cave and wigwam, for centuries." She sighed. "But the new whites, when they finally came, colonists, empire builders, they were a different matter."

"That's exactly what I mean," Julian began.

"Be a listener today, Capricorn, and learn a little." She winked and got solemn. "Tell them, baby."

Frieda spoke up, another of her stories. "The outsiders started showing up in these valleys four hundred years ago, the French, then the English, and from the beginning we saw that they were too much like us, aggressors, a conquering people. And they had us outnumbered, of course, so we stayed underground, in our caves, at first, pretending to be Choctaws ourselves, in our beads and our stained skin and hair and our ceremonial feathers. The French explorers, the settlers at Vincennes and Terre Haute, never knew the difference. As camouflage, we pretended to be converted to Christianity, by Jesuits in the French expeditions . . ."

Fat Mama couldn't keep quiet any longer. "But under the disguise of that Jesuitical bullshit and a pinch or two, later, of Holy-Roller hellfire hysteria, we stayed as we always were, worshipers of the Great Mother and the Unconquered Sun."

Julian breathed out a sigh like a long moan. Fat Mama smiled and rubbed his head.

Frieda picked up the story again, with scarcely a pause. "But the hardest time was when they opened up the Indiana Territory to farming, and the white settlers came in like hungry locusts, on muleback from the East, by flatboat down the rivers, and we could see they meant to grab it all. We needed a new masquerade, a new adaptation, so family by family we shed our eagle feathers and put on coonskin caps, and blended into the foliage again. We abandoned our runes, learned English, and entered our claims at the land offices. Meanwhile, we dug the local limestone and built the fortress-church on the hill and the secret underground passages. And we kept the strangers out. One way or another—ostracism, boycotts, threats—we made them unwelcome, and they always moved on. So by the time of the Revolution, we were an old pioneer community, and by then we had long since held our services and bled our bulls in the new sanctuary in the church."

She paused. Fat Mama went on with the story. "And by that time, after the death of many cycles of priests, our people only half remembered that a few centuries earlier we were still cave dwellers, and they had lost the secret passageways down to our ancient Sanctum and its treasure, somewhere in the labyrinths of our oldest home."

Her big eyes rolled with satisfaction as she reached the end of the tale. "Only half remembered, that is, except for a special line of women who had learned to distrust the mercenary priests—the anointed women who had been, generation after generation, the keepers of the inn, as well as what we had always been in this rough continent, and back to the Viking memories of our icebound northern people—mothers of the earth."

Julian was smiling now, his eyes half closed. He reached for her hand and fondled it, and when he spoke it was as if he were somewhere else, a long way off. "So," he murmured, "the process survives, claiming its ritual sacrifice. Long live the survivors." He seemed at peace with himself, something Frank had never seen, hadn't expected. "After all," Julian went on, his voice dreamy, "we're all really Vikings, aren't we, from sea to shining sea? No wonder we're feared and hated everywhere. What people has ever plundered the world as we have? Who has ever been swifter, greedier, more unscrupulous? Who else ever dreamed of the thousand-horsepower car?"

"Oh, come on." Frank's nervousness wouldn't go away, and he was getting more and more irritable, impatient at his uncle's instant theorizing.

"And not only that, we celebrate all those other dark mysteries, too, celebrate them in our hearts, those fears and desires visited upon our souls by a million lives we still live without having lived them, those thoughts, dreams, wild urges. How did you know, Frank, how to kill that bull?"

Fat Mama and Frieda were nodding. Frank toyed with the daisy, refused to accept. "All right, all right, talk that way if you want, make it just another quick hypothesis. But there's more to it than that, or a lot less. I mean, we saw the gold, the black stone, the altar. It's all down there."

"Is it?" Julian smiled. "Five hundred feet of limestone. That was a pretty considerable quake. Look at the cracks in these walls, look at the ceilings. Chances are, most of the caves around here are blocked off. The gold, the skeleton, the long ship, all buried. Wong's—that is, Olaf's—parchments, burned."

"But I know it's down there. We all do."

Julian shrugged. "If a tree falls, deep in the forest . . ."

"What are you getting at?"

"Killing the bull was a moment of truth for you, whether you knew it then or not. It changed your life, decided it. And killing Magnus was another."

"I didn't kill him, I dusted him off with a rock." But Frank knew a quibble when he heard it.

Julian pondered. "We all know how to kill our fathers, that's nothing new. What's interesting is that apparently we also know how to bury our kings and gods. What does that mean?" For some reason he seemed uncertain, unusual for him. "There's so much truth swirling around us here that I'm not really sure myself."

Frieda nodded. "Truth converges."

"What's that?" Julian was instantly alert, sharp-edged.

"You just said it yourself. Implied it, I mean." She was defensive, taken aback by Julian's abruptness. "Truth converges."

Fat Mama patted Frieda's hand. "We Hoosiers say that sometimes, Capricorn. An old saw."

Julian was triumphant. "Yes, of course you would, of course you'd say that! Truth, my God, it drifts around you here like sand on a beach! Iron filings . . . What happens to a plate of iron filings held over a magnet?"

Frank humored him: "They magnetize, align themselves along the magnetic field, map out the lines of force."

"And if you move the magnet?"

"The filings re-sort themselves around it, a new diagram."

"And that's the pattern of history, the trick of mythology, the sleight of hand of all religions, superstitions—truth converges. No, better yet, all truth converges in all places." Julian plopped his hands on his knees as if he'd just settled everything. "So of course we're among Vikings here, and of course you killed the bull like Mithra and cast the avenging stone at Magnus, for of course the father must be killed and the god-king must die, must die again and again, to atone for us all and to raise us up in an always recurring spring."

Oh, he was happy all right. Nonsense or not, he was clearly happy: surrounded by scrambled eggs, sweet rolls, and sausages, Julian had stopped eating.

It was time, then. Frank took a deep breath and spoke his challenge. "Julian, I've made up my mind. I'm giving up the partnership, the business, all of that. Moving on. To do something honest, and get that agent off my tail."

"Are you sure he's on your tail?"

"Am I sure?" Frank sputtered, went speechless.

"Sometimes we invent our nemesis, knowing we need one."

"That's ridiculous." Frank set forth the challenge again, eager to meet something head-on, not end in this clutter of uncertainties. "Anyway, I mean it. I'm quitting for good." He had broken with Julian at last. He didn't need him any more.

And not needing him, Frank discovered something else: he would miss Julian, really miss him.

Julian smiled. "Good for you. By the way, I'm quitting our little racket, too. Permanently, I mean. I just decided."

Frank felt empty, and a little foolish. He had hurled himself against a door and found it open. "You are?"

"Don't really need the money, and it's not that much fun any more. So I'll wrap things up with Nancy at the office—for both of us, if you like. Eventually."

"OK, Julian." He hesitated, embarrassed. "Thanks."

Julian coughed. "It's a moment of truth for me, too. To be alive means having to change, as Sybil says. I think I'll just hang around Ash Garden for a while, maybe go on a crash diet, and after I lose a few pounds, try a little spelunking."

Frank squinted at him. "Is it true, then, what Olaf thought? Were you really only after the gold?"

"Oh, come, my boy, come, come." He patted Fat Mama fondly. She laughed her musical baritone.

Frieda kissed her mother. "We won't be tending the lamp any more, now that the holy treasure's lost. So I'm going with Frank, Mama. I suppose the world needs saving out there as much as it does here at home."

For the first time, Frank heard a note of self-mockery in her voice. Eighteen years old: she was growing up.

She stuck the wilted daisy in Frank's hair and hugged him. Indiana moved slowly eastward on its long axis.

Somewhere far off there were gunshots. Fat Mama jumped up and lunged to the door, and the three others followed. Down the long slope of the street they saw a crowd in blue uniforms, moving forward in undulating waves, rippling along the sidewalk.

Frieda whispered, "The sea will rise up."

Frank thought he saw a snap-brimmed hat bobbing along at the edge of the shifting mass, but in the confusion he couldn't be sure. Had he really invented the agents himself, right from the start?

He heard Frieda's voice, cool but intense. "They want you to be God, Frank."

Then he heard chanting. "O God our king!" came the wavering roar, like breakers on a distant beach. "O king our savior!"

"You get the message, Frank?" Fat Mama was talking fast. "Magnus must have set this up before he came after us. There's only one thing you can do now, and that's run. Take advantage of new horizons, both of you, act quickly but not rashly. Frieda, call me as soon as you can. Now go."

She was firm, but tears were trickling down her face, streams in the fertile land.

Frieda kissed her, then kissed Julian, who beamed. She fretted a moment. "Will you be safe, Mama?"

"Of course I will. It's not me or Julian they're after. Hurry!"

The Stingray roared at the first twist of the key, and Frank bulled his way into the heavy traffic, leaving the two bulky figures at the curb, arm in arm, waving goodbye.

The mob was only a hundred yards behind, and as the Stingray slipped away, Frank saw them in the rearview mirror, running after the car, coming faster than he could drive through the dense traffic. Soon they'd be on them, smashing the windows, yanking open the doors, pulling them into the street . . .

He took the only way out. Holding the horn, with headlights and blinkers on, he pulled into the oncoming traffic and pressed down on the accelerator. Cars squeezed over in a panic, making a narrow fifth lane, through which the Stingray glided perilously.

In spite of the danger, Frieda was smiling a blurry triumph. "It's not a gift, Frank, we've earned it. You understand now, you understand everything." She put a hand on his knee, laughing. Her happiness crept up his skin and into his chest: anything was possible.

Frank took a deep, deliberate breath. He had already had enough of the fifth lane. With a few hundred yards between him and the pursuers, he risked the regular traffic again. Cars veered away from the menacing Stingray. It purred through a little island of space.

Free . . . Free?

And now what? Back home again? To the fierce harmonies of sirens and horns, to the fragrance of crosstown buses, to the vision of Broadway, gridlocked? Well, what else? Light out for the territories? The world was all before them.

Together.

"Which way, Frieda?"

She glanced at her grimy hands and smiled at him. "West," she said, "young man." She touched his cheek, and he felt green shoots in the fresh-turned earth.

Spring, she had said, *is in the mind, and we are all love has.*

Love kept his accelerator foot heavy. He took minor risks, sliding through stoplights, passing on yellow lines, daring fenders on both sides, making good time, driving out past trailer courts and shopping centers, past factories and filling stations, and away, away, to the West.

Together.

To some haven in the open country, to the music of clear water, to singing birds? To puffy white clouds in a jewel of a sky, to bright flowers in rolling meadows?

Of course not. Off in the reddening afternoon, to another Ash Garden, and then another, and yet another, and still again another, past poisoned fields and toxic dumps and dying rivers, pressing on, O pioneers, until they reached that great oil slick in the West, where sunsets gleam rainbow-colored on the vast and greasy surface.

Going there together.